THE FALL OF MAN

By the same author:

SEEING THINGS

(for children)
THE BLINDFOLD TRACK
SECRETS
DEAR COMRADE
A KNOT OF SPELLS
ZAK

THE FALL OF MAN

Frances Thomas

LONDON
VICTOR GOLLANCZ LTD
1989

First published in Great Britain 1989
by Victor Gollancz Ltd,
14 Henrietta Street, London WC2E 8QJ

British Library Cataloguing in Publication Data
Thomas, Frances, *1943*–
    The fall of man.
    I. Title
    823'.914[F]
    ISBN 0–575–04475–6

Typeset at The Spartan Press Ltd,
Lymington, Hants
and printed in Great Britain by
St Edmundsbury Press Ltd, Bury St Edmunds, Suffolk

THE FALL OF MAN

Chapter 1

At the station Daniel found there was no one to meet him.

No one!

Of course, it was bloody obvious, wasn't it, from the letter; all that stuff about 'caring community' and 'warm family atmosphere'. It was obvious that when it came to the point, they would simply let him down.

People did let people down, all the time. You didn't have to travel to the wilds of Wales to find *that* out. All the way from — what was the name of the silly place — Welwyn was it, or Watford? — he'd been worried that they simply weren't up to it . . . Mr John Hunter. *Mister* John bloody Hunter, indeed. What a shambles. What a . . .

But now here he was at the station, all alone, in the middle of bloody nowhere.

First a dingy Inter-City, smelling of ancient sandwiches, had taken him to Birmingham. Birmingham might have been Hell. People pushed and shoved; on the floor was a half-eaten chicken take-away and a sanded patch of vomit. Birmingham sent him to Shrewsbury, where they made him wait an hour on the platform, under a bust set high into the wall and called, simply, Howard. Not Howard anything, or anything Howard, just Howard. Typical.

Well, Shrewsbury eventually did manage to come up with a train, a train so small and primitive that it was more like a bus on wheels. Apart from the time in France when his father went down with an ulcer, he had never really been in the country before. The enormity of it all struck him. There was so much of everything; grass, hills, trees, that sort of stuff, and it was so . . . so unrestrained.

Oh, look here, he could go mad in the country, he could really go over the edge.

Then they'd all be sorry, wouldn't they?

From Shrewsbury the train entered a long sweep of silent valley, a country of soft, densely packed hills, so suffused with sunlight that the green turned to gold; where bronze pheasants strutted in creamy stubble, buzzards coasted on high thermals; where giants slumbered in their hillside graves and the ghost of a Roman road slipped in and out of the track and beneath village streets, only their names — Stretton and Street and Stratford — sometimes whispering its presence. The train stopped at tiny stations where milk churns and marigolds waited in the sun. It was a land so deep and hidden that Daniel should have felt all the excitement of a first explorer.

Instead he began to panic. In fact, panic was an old friend; he used it like a prophylactic, as though feeling it would keep all the really bad stuff at bay. If you didn't panic, the monsters would certainly get you.

Only panic hadn't held back the monsters this summer. The trick hadn't worked at all. The panic that overtook him before Finals was a nasty, mean, slimy kind of panic that wrapped its way round the brain and clogged the blood. He could not think properly, or work, or even remember simple things, like where he kept the coffee or put his socks. He did not tell anyone about this feeling, not even his parents, though he had never kept things from them before.

It wasn't a breakdown. The rosy-faced counsellor from the Student Health Service had been most insistent about that. A hiccup, a sneeze, a temporary set back. A few weeks' rest and everything would be as right as rain.

No, it wasn't a breakdown. They were all sure of that.

8

But if not, then what the hell was it?

And what was John bloody Hunter going to do about it?

Daniel would have been crosser still if he had known that there, travelling with him on the train from Shrewsbury, was that very Celia Hunter who should have been there at Llanafon to meet him. They did not — why should they? — notice each other. She, pale, freckled, distracted, in her sandals and drab flower-printed skirt, leaned back against her seat, shopping gathered around her. Oh, God, she thought, as the little train lurched and swayed, what have I done, what have I done? She thought of Hunter standing by the kitchen window blocking out the light. 'Celia, my dear old thing,' he was saying, 'can't you, just for once, get things straight?' When Hunter stood like that, she could not move, or think. Words dried up on her lips, her brain froze.

The train drew into Llanafon, with hotels called The Metropole and The Commodore and round the station, fretwork like lace on the edge of a traycloth. Daniel got out of the train, as did an ageing hippy couple with their baby, a farmer with a russet outdoor face, a woman carrying sweet peas in her shopping bag and Celia Hunter.

Celia, not noticing the stranded Daniel, hurried away. She had left the children with Janet Barber in Claerwen Road. Would Rose have wet her knickers? Would Amos have bitten Wayne Barber? There were no cornflakes for breakfast, but she wouldn't have enough money if she were to get Hunter's muesli, and all she could do for supper tonight was cauliflower cheese; Joseph would turn his nose up at that, ever so politely, of course . . .

But then, coming out of Spar, she saw a young man in a heavy sweater and though he was really nothing like, something about the slope of his shoulders made her stand still and forget all these domestic matters. Jamie, she thought with a sudden rush to the heart, oh, Jamie . . .

★

The train pulled away, the station emptied. A porter crossed the line and disappeared behind a door on the opposite platform. A window marked 'Enquiries' had been firmly shut. Daniel looked at a poster — it said, 'Off-peak travel: Take A Copy,' but there was nothing to take. Another proclaimed, '*His Blood Will Wash Your Sins Away. Worship with Us at the Fellowship Meeting House.*' Somewhere there must be a bakery for he could smell fresh spiced bread. There was no traffic.

And John bloody Hunter had not sent anyone to meet him!

'St Rhuna?' said the porter, who, God, must have been about a hundred and five. 'You want St Rhuna, do you?'

'Yes, they were supposed to send somebody, but . . .'

'It's a good old step. I don't think you'd walk it.'

'No, I know, but they were going to send . . .'

'Isn't it, Walter?' the porter called out to a man in a tweed jacket leaning against an ancient Land Rover, who, with his foxy, predatory face, yellow teeth and mouldering jacket, seemed to be in the process of some slow fungal decomposition.

'Wanted me, did you, Tom?' he said.

'I was telling this gentleman here it's a good step to St Rhuna's.'

'They . . . Disserth House . . . Mr Hunter was supposed to be sending . . .' Daniel said.

'Disserth? They won't send anyone. Get up. I'll take you.'

What? Into a car with a strange man and a smelly one, too, by the looks of him? He could not possibly do such a thing. 'Er . . . thank you very much,' he said, getting into the Land Rover.

The man called Walter drove silently, and much too fast, through narrow lanes. Hedges swayed and joined overhead, brambles wound savage coils like barbed-wire fences.

Then suddenly, as if slashed by an enchanted sword, the hedges vanished and they were on top of a wide open space where yellow lichen spread over fallen drystone and the bones of the hill showed like protruding shoulder blades through the cropped, jewel-bright grass. On each bend the Land Rover bounced in the air and Daniel — there were no visible seat-belts — bounced too. At one point, Walter swerved violently to avoid a sheep. 'Daft buggers, sheep,' he said, as Daniel's head settled slowly back on to his shoulders, 'and I should know.'

At a rusty old petrol station with nettles growing around the pumps, they came to a fork in the road and a bridge. Walter took the smaller of the two roads. Before them was now a high, bleak hill, almost a mountain, its bare red-tawny slope glowing with an eerie witched radiance. King Arthur or a faerie enchantress with white-gold tresses might have lain snoring in such a hill. Walter braked abruptly. 'Here's where I go. You go on there, left.'

'Oh,' said Daniel.

'Well, you didn't expect to be dropped right outside the door, did you? This is the country, boy, not a bloody London taxi.'

Daniel, knowing he was being made a fool of, got down meekly, but raging inwardly. 'Half mile,' Walter said with a grin. 'Give or take. First house you come to. White gate on your left. Can't miss her.'

Then, in a flurry of dust and gravel, he was gone.

Daniel, alone in the silent road, clutched his suitcase and looked around him. He thought of stories he had heard of murders, of bodies left to bloat and peel in ditches, of ghosts and goblins and Welsh Nationalists.

Half a mile! Oh, damn, damn, damn, *damn* the country-side!

At last there was a gate. It was smaller than he thought it would be and it was not white, but faded blue, set deep amid speckled laurels. Still, it was a garden gate, man-made. He found this reassuring.

He pushed it. It creaked softly, but would not let him in. He pushed again and this time it moved slightly. The top hinge had come loose and the gate hit the ground, excavating a semi-circular trough through leaf-mould. Before him, a little path led down and down, through dark and secret evergreens, ranked like a mass of green spears. The air settled itself calmly around him, as in a church; the compost shifted and stirred at his feet; dark sprays brushed his cheek. Only a few pale rays of sun came through the leaves and there was no birdsong.

He had a vague sensation that the path led downwards, but it was not until it suddenly stopped and sunlight rushed at him that he could see where he was. He was standing on a green slope, overlooking a deeply scoured valley through which a tiny stream was hurtling noisily. First it rushed over stones, then spread out smoothly in a wide arc upon which the sun glittered hectically. And there, standing in the water, was a naked girl.

Impossible! And shocking. He could hardly believe what he saw, but he blinked and still she was there! She stood in the stream, turned towards, but not seeing him, arms behind her head, face raised in ecstasy to the sky. Her body made a long, sinuous, silvery curve; she was like a statue, but she was not a statue. He could see the slight sway as she braced herself against the current at her feet, the lifting of her hair in the wind. As for her face, or even the colour of her hair, he could not see it; the fierce sun blotted out all detail.

Impossible . . . but there she was, and still she did not move except for the gentle rocking as she kept her balance in the water. Perhaps he stood there for no more than a few seconds, but it felt like longer. *Quite impossible* . . . yet there was never a trick of the light like this. Oh, she was there all right.

He backed away into the wood, dazed. He, Daniel Green, had seen a naked girl! A girl with nothing on! Quite . . . bare! She was there and he had seen her!

For the thing was, although he was twenty years old, he had never thought very much about girls till now, even clothed ones. What was important were your books and your models and your stamp collection. Of course, he knew the facts of life — his mother the Professor had seen to that. But it was all rather like learning some obscure language that you would never be called upon to use. Until now.

Now he suddenly saw what it might all be about.

Dreadful!

But the thing was, it wasn't really dreadful at all. Really, it was rather nice. In fact, the more he thought about it, the more it seemed like just the thing to be doing.

Nevertheless, he didn't stand watching for very long. He thought that that must surely be against the rules. So after a few moments, leaving her, oblivious and stretching her white arms to the sun, he returned to the path through the undergrowth, which he charged through with renewed fervour, invigorated, strong, the prince in the fairy-tale.

And now, in the distance, he could see the gables and chimneys of what must surely be Disserth House.

Soon the undergrowth cleared and he was in a garden. Beyond lawns and paths was an old house sunk deep into the ground; its roof was of tumbled indigo slates, the walls of creeper-covered stone. It was not beautiful, for the muddle of too many centuries had cluttered and confused the frontage. One generation had tacked on a heavy porch, another an arched Gothic window. There was a prim Victorian bay on the ground floor and the twentieth century had supplied a hideous breezeblock extension. But the thick creeper softened the lines and a tumble of white roses fell around the door.

13

At the door, which was ajar, he called, 'Hallo.' Muddy Wellingtons lined the porch and there was a child's rusty bicycle. 'Hallo.'

He peered into the hall, and then, more boldly, stepped inside over the threshold to worn and sunken flagstones. Dark perspectives glinted before him; there was glittering granite-coloured light from the floor, the sheen of undulating walls, with doors closed, or mysteriously half open. Framed by the door, everything shone and glowed richly; a polished chest with a copper jug of marigolds, a strip of Indian rug, a curve of balustrade.

At the end of the corridor was a glass-panelled door. As he watched, light from a source of sunlight beyond it turned it into a sheet of flaming bronze. He half expected a voice to say, 'Take off your shoes: this is holy ground.'

Then the door opened and out stepped Jehovah himself.

Well, he *looked* like Jehovah: huge and well constructed with a halo of flaming white hair and a beard. Though he was not actually wearing white robes, an expansive white T-shirt gave that impression. His bulk filled the doorway. He loomed, he towered. Daniel knew that here at last was the famous John Hunter.

'Who on earth . . .?' said John Hunter.

'Green, sir. Daniel Green.' Daniel automatically used the voice he would have used to a teacher.

'Green? Green? Tomorrow, surely.'

'Today.'

John Hunter clapped a huge hand to his huge head and went back into the kitchen to return thumbing through a calendar. 'Today? Today? Green. Good lord, so it is! Good lord!'

'Thursday,' Daniel said a little smugly.

'Thursday it is. We thought . . . Celia said Friday. Good lord, what a cock-up.'

Daniel's parents never used bad language. He said, 'Sorry, sir.'

14

'Don't apologize, Daniel. It isn't your mistake, is it?'

'I knew it was Thursday,' said Daniel, humbly but secretly pleased. 'The letter said.'

'What could Celia have been thinking of? Never mind. You're here. How *did* you get here, by the way?'

'This bloke gave me a lift, Walter Something. He's got a farm near here.'

'Walter? Oh, *Walter Jones!* Sooner you than me. Still, let's go and have a cup of tea and then we'll get your case up to your room. Oh, and by the way, don't call me sir, for God's sake. Everyone calls me Hunter, just Hunter. Well now, I'll lead the way and you can recover from your ordeal.'

Ordeal? Did he mock? But his clear blue eyes — explorer's blue, cricket captain's blue — twinkled. Daniel followed him through a low doorway. The room was dark and full of shadows. Shockingly, one of the shadows moved and breathed out just in front of him. Then he saw that it was not a shadow but a face, a very black face. His eyes became accustomed to the darkness, and he saw that the face was plump and amiable. The voice that came from it was deep and well modulated with perfect BBC diction.

'Ah, Hunter. Do we have a new guest?'

'Joe, this is Daniel, Daniel Green. Joseph. Joseph Agbodeka.'

Joseph Agbodeka bowed from the waist and told Daniel that it was a pleasure to make his acquaintance. 'But I understood . . . did I not understand . . . tomorrow?'

'Dear old Celia. Her mistake.'

'Oh, dear. Poor Celia. How we leave everything to her.'

'We do indeed,' said Hunter. 'We expect perfection, but then no human being is perfect. Daniel, some tea?'

'Please,' Joseph said with a mocking bow, 'allow me. Tea is the sacred nectar of Disserth House, Daniel.'

Hunter smiled, his strong perfect teeth gleaming white. 'How they tease me, Daniel. But they all tolerate my little ways most kindly.'

'Of course,' Joseph said. 'Are we not your obedient children?'

'Heavens, Daniel, do put your suitcase down. Sit down. Sit down.'

Hunter pointed to an ancient armchair and Daniel fell into the middle of what seemed to be a hole surrounded by springs. There was a huge old fireplace that went deep into the thick wall, oak beams and a wide wooden window-sill; but there was also vinyl wallpaper with a pattern of turquoise flowers screaming the length of the fireplace wall, polyester curtains and a carpet patterned with vivid swirls. Bits of furniture lay around like a museum of twentieth-century bad taste — imitation leather from the sixties, orange moquette with wooden arms from the fifties, a streamlined sideboard from the thirties and a spindly, gilt-legged coffee table from goodness knows when. Newspapers and Lego bricks were scattered everywhere. On the mantelpiece was a tall can of hairspray and a pink brush clogged with a flurry of blonde hairs.

Nevertheless, as Hunter sat opposite him in the leatherette chair, there was something very reassuring about him; that solid well-filled bulk, that white head, that perfection of skin and teeth. Such a person could not possibly let you down. Daniel began to forget about the station. Hunter was most positively, most definitely *there*.

There, too, was Joseph Agbodeka, who now came in with the tea tray, smiling and bowing with that mock humility which seemed to suggest quite the opposite. What was he here for anyway? What had he done? For, as in a prison, you surely had to have done something to end up here. What did that bowing charm conceal? And why must he smile so much?

Joseph, still smiling, put the tray down on the coffee table. 'I could find no biscuits, I'm afraid.'

'Oh, what nonsense, Joseph. There's a whole tin of Celia's oatmeal specials somewhere. You can't have looked.'

'I *looked*,' said Joseph, 'but clearly I did not *see*. Milk, Daniel? Sugar? You must admit, Hunter, that since coming to Disserth House I have become a very proficient pourer of tea. For a humble African, raised on banana stew, this is no mean achievement, I think.'

'You wouldn't think, would you, from listening to him, Daniel, that Joseph is really an Ashanti prince.'

'A minor branch,' said Joseph humbly. 'A minor branch.'

'Of course, here at Disserth House, we pay very little attention to background. To us, everyone is a prince. But it's nice to know these things sometimes. Joseph, did you know that Daniel's parents are both very eminent professors at London University?'

Joseph came over to Daniel with a teacup and at the same time endeavoured to shake his hand, a complicated manoeuvre that involved Daniel in some difficult passing across and over of hands.

'I congratulate you,' said Joseph, when he had finally managed it. 'This is the true aristocracy, the aristocracy of the intellect.' Daniel looked at his tea in embarrassment. 'You see,' went on Joseph, 'in Ghana we aristocrats are ten for a penny. But in England — ah, in England — the name of Prince stands for something. After all, if I remember rightly, there are three of them — Prince Charles, Andrew and Edward.' He began to stir his tea, but then looked up. 'And, of course, Princess Michael of Kent, so also a Prince Michael. And Princess Anne, so doubtless a Prince Anne. Ah, I am such a fan of your Royal Family! And how we all thrilled to the love story of . . .'

'Oh, Joseph! You don't give a shit about the Royal Family!' A girl had just come into the room. Daniel turned to see her and then almost spilled his tea. She was blonde, with a skimpy cotton dress.

And her hair was wet.

'Ah, Dorothy,' Hunter said, 'I was looking for you just now.'

17

'I was in the garden. *Trying* to dry my hair. She's nicked my hair drier again.'

'*She*, Dorothy?'

'You know who I mean. Celia.'

'This is Dorothy, my elder daughter,' said Hunter. 'Normally,' he added sternly, 'she's nicer than this.'

'No, I'm not,' said Dorothy. She yawned.

'And this is Daniel, Dorothy. He's just arrived.'

Dorothy turned a full, unblinking stare upon Daniel. She had a pretty, slightly pinched and crumpled little face, not unlike a Labrador puppy, with small, dark eyes.

Daniel, meanwhile, watched her open-mouthed.

'Are you all right, Daniel?' said Hunter.

'Oh, yes. Just a bit . . . er . . . sleepy.'

'The air of the hills,' Joseph said solicitously. 'It is most soporific. But after a while, Daniel, the body adjusts and you become a hill dweller.'

'Dorothy, darling, why not show Daniel the garden before he goes up to his room? The fresh air might do him good.'

'You always call me darling,' Dorothy said, 'when you want me to do something boring.'

'Look, it's all right,' Daniel said, 'I wouldn't want to . . .'

Dorothy threw him a scornful glance. 'I didn't mean you boring. I meant the garden boring. All right, Darren, come on.'

'Daniel, actually.'

'Off you both go,' Hunter said. He smiled as he spoke, but his tone brooked no disagreement.

Daniel followed Dorothy out into the garden.

Chapter 2

'Ah,' Hunter said. 'Methinks I see my late espoused saint.'

'I'm sorry,' Celia said. 'First the car wouldn't start and then Janet . . .'

Celia was now surrounded by her children, Amos, Rose and Charlie, squirming around and tugging at her. 'Daddy Daddy Daddy,' Amos cried, 'we had lollipops.' Lollipops were forbidden at Disserth House.

'My dear Celia, even had the car started at once, you would still have been too late. You forgot a guest.'

'A guest?'

'Our young Master Green. Daniel Green to be precise.'

'*Daniel Green?*'

'There's certainly nothing wrong with your hearing, Celia.'

'But he's tomorrow, surely.'

'Today,' Hunter said in the mildest of tones. 'Just look in the calendar, my sweet.'

'And then,' said Amos, sniffing the perilous air, 'we had pink ice-cream with crunchy bits . . .'

'I'm so sorry, I don't . . .'

'And we saw television *all day*. There was this fight and this man went . . .'

'Daddy, did you know,' said Charlie, 'that the sun is shrinking and in three billion years Daddy . . .'

'How did he . . . is he all right?'

'No thanks to anyone here. Our friend Walter Jones brought him.'

'Oh, help,' said Celia. 'I'd better start getting supper.'

'Splendid,' said Hunter. 'And what joys are in store for us tonight, may we ask?'

'I was going to make cauliflower cheese, if that's . . .'

'Don't like cauliflower,' said Amos. He gave a tentative sniff, looked around, and then launched into a full-blown wail. 'I hate CAULIFLOWER MUMMY I HATE . . .'

'Shut up,' said Charlie scornfully. 'We had tea. We're not having cauliflower.'

'*Cauliflower cheese*?' said Hunter. 'Is that the best you can do for someone's first night?'

'I thought his first night was tomorrow, and I was going to do spaghetti tomorrow.'

'Hardly an improvement, Celia.'

'But I've only got twelve pounds left . . .'

'My dear,' said Hunter with the utmost gentleness, 'if you can't manage your housekeeping . . .'

'Why can't we have television?' Amos asked.

Celia answered mechanically, 'Because it's bad for you.' Hunter said, 'Because, my boy, if you watch television all the time you miss the good things of life.'

'But there was this man Daddy Daddy there was this man and there was this lady and he went bang bang and it was all blood and . . .'

Celia vanished into the kitchen in some relief, leaving Hunter to explain the evils of violence to Amos. She closed the kitchen door behind her and rested her palms on the rim of the sink, looking out of the window to where Dorothy and an as yet unknown boy scrambled down the hilly slopes of the garden. She gave a deep sigh that had little to do with overdrafts and cauliflower. As she sighed, she mouthed, but did not say out loud, the name that was in her thoughts.

In a way, you could say it had all been Hunter's fault. For if he had not so readily volunteered her to do the washing up at the Old Folk's Supper then what passed between her and Jamie at lunch might never have come to anything and left only a faint pleasant memory behind.

Was it only two weeks ago? For that was the day of the Loftuses' lunch party. Norman Loftus the vicar was celebrating his sixtieth birthday and Deirdre had arranged a party on the vicarage lawn.

It was a glorious day; one of those days when the sun licks away all the slaty Puritan greyness of Wales and transforms it into an enchanted green and golden land. The vicarage was an undistinguished house on the edge of the next village (St Rhuna's shared its vicar with the inhabitants of Llatho a couple of miles up the road), but that day the sun poured down like honey and everything looked beautiful.

Deirdre whisked the children away to a table of their own where they scoffed and squabbled happily, sparing Celia the usual tuggings and clingings around her legs. Today Celia was allowed to be a human being. 'Sorry to be a bore,' said Deirdre, 'but I've stuck you next to Jamie, poor lamb; all us old fogies, no one his own . . . but he thinks the *world* of you and you've always been *so* nice; such a pity none of his own friends but you *don't* mind, do you?'

She did mind, at first, just a bit, for though Jamie at twenty-three, just finishing a post-graduate degree at Bristol University, was no longer a child, it did feel rather like being used as baby-sitter. These days, Hunter left most of the emotional messes of his guests for Celia to sort out and she was tired of the frantic solipsism of the young, and what seemed like their perpetual self-pity. So she steeled herself to a lunchtime stuck with the problems of Jamie Loftus.

It wasn't the first time they'd talked; once, when he was thirteen, she'd found him almost reduced to tears by some maths homework. 'Frightful stuff, maths,' Hunter said with his usual breeziness and went off to look at some apple

21

trees in the vicarage garden. But Celia, who had been good at maths at school, found that she remembered how to do the problem and so she was able to explain it to Jamie. For a long while, they sat side by side, her head nearly brushing his. At the end, he smiled shyly down with a smile of pure joy. 'Thank you, Mrs Hunter. I could never have done it without you.' 'Oh rubbish,' she said. 'Anyhow, do call me Celia, for goodness' sake.' Though he'd responded in the awkward way of the young by not calling her anything thereafter.

Now, at the head of the table, Norman Loftus beamed, silver-haired, long-nosed, imposing. Norman made you feel that the world would always have a place for vicars, that vicars were at the focus of life, just as they were at the focus of villages. There could be, thought Celia, no ragged ends, no loose bricks in a life like Norman's. 'Jolly good, jolly good,' he said smiling round genially. 'And how noble of you to turn out for a decrepit old man like myself. Well, what more is there to say but lead on Macduff, and cursed be he, et cetera!'

'Now, don't stand on ceremony, *please*, anyone, just help yourselves, everybody grab, don't bother to be polite.'

'Of course, in spite of what Mama says, no one will do any such thing,' came Jamie's voice by her side and it startled her, who had not spoken to him for some time, to find how it had deepened and grown firm. 'Mrs Hunter, let me spare you from the fearful necessity of having to grab. Do have some wine.'

'Oh, do call me Celia,' she said, as she had said before, and this time he rewarded her with a direct smile. 'Celia,' he said, as he poured sweet warm white wine into her glass. Further along the table, Hunter was seated next to an old sparring partner of his, a Catholic priest who ran a retreat near Llanafon. There was nothing Hunter liked more than a good argument on the Incarnation, and Father Glass would always oblige with one. Hunter would not take any notice of her for the rest of the afternoon. Celia began to relax a little, and leaned back in her chair, sipping her wine.

Next to her, Jamie reached across the table for the bowl of salad, the sun burnishing the reddish hairs on his freckled arms. In appearance and colouring he was, in fact, not dissimilar to Celia; you might have taken them for brother and sister. And he was unlike any of the young people she was used to; there was something gravely old-fashioned in Jamie Loftus's demeanour, something out of key with the modern world, as though he were a throw-back to a slightly earlier generation, one of the bright-eyed, courteous young men of the pre-war era, with their short haircuts and conventional clothes, their bracing enthusiasms undiminished by the need to be cool. She returned his smile, for the pleasure of feeling that attentive, serious regard upon her. She was not consciously flirting; Celia did not think she knew how to flirt, with the result that she returned more to him than perhaps was wise for a married mother of three. As the afternoon advanced, the world around her seemed to recede as though she and Jamie were alone in a bubble. They talked about everything and nothing; he did not scoff when she spoke of her feelings, he did not seek to grind her ideas to dust, but listened as though she were the most fascinating person in the world, returning her small confidences with ones of his own. By the time Deirdre brought tea and cakes, Celia was, though she did not know it, lost.

Still, under the circumstances, it was unlikely that anything would have followed, if later on, Hunter hadn't offered her to help with that washing up. 'Oh, I'm sure Celia will be delighted to lend a hand, won't you, Celia?' Deirdre accepted with delight. 'Oh, Celia, *so* kind, I have beastly old choir Thursdays worst luck and Norman'll be in Hereford and washing up isn't really his you know anyway so it would just be Jamie on his own, poor I mean he's *frightfully* keen but it's a bit *you* know, isn't it?'

Well, so that was how she and Jamie had found themselves all alone in the church hall along with the debris of twenty servings of pork with apple sauce and twenty sherry trifles. The strange thing was how stiff and self-conscious they were, after the relaxation of the birthday lunch, how awkwardly both moved around, apologizing and not looking each other in the eyes as they moved piles of dirty plates. 'Sorry,' Jamie had said once too often as he brushed her shoulder. And 'sorry,' she had replied with unnecessary humility. Jamie put down his pile of plates. 'Oh, God, Celia,' he said, in a leaden voice. She froze, her hand half-way towards a tea-towel. 'It's no use,' he went on, 'I'm making a bloody fool of myself.' 'What do you mean?' she muttered. 'Oh, Celia, Celia, it's just that I . . . oh God, why don't you tell me to get lost. . . ?'

She did not, of course. Though little happened that first night beyond incoherent mumblings and hasty embraces, things moved fast; they arranged to meet the following week, on one of the rare days that Hunter allowed her to catch up with essential shopping in Shrewsbury. Jamie was there, waiting for her as she got off the train, and he shadowed her like a ghost while she bought socks and vests and T-shirts, cramming her entire day's shopping into a twenty minute dash. Then, in Deirdre's car, they drove deep into the Shropshire countryside, and in a quiet field several hours had sped by as if they were no time at all; and now it was too late for any going back.

'Well, here are the chickens,' said Dorothy. 'I told you they were boring.' Were they? They were fat and busy and looked cross. Something about their sheeny bronze feathers reminded him of old ladies' clothes. 'I don't know anything about chickens,' he said lamely.

'There's nothing to know,' she replied in scorn. 'They go cluck cluck and they lay smelly eggs covered in shit which Celia keeps trying to shove down my throat. Ugh!

24

Gross! Can you imagine eating *eggs*? It's like eating dead babies.'

'Well, not quite . . .'

'They even have bits of blood in them sometimes, and you know what that means, don't you; it means the chicken's got the curse and they expect you to *eat* it. Mind, Celia's cooking is pretty foul anyway. Have you met Celia yet?'

'No. She was supposed to meet . . .'

'Oh, you will. She's Hunter's wife. Hunter's had lots of wives. My mum was his second. She went off with an accountant. We are not,' she said, assuming a Voice, 'supposed-to-talk-about-it. But what the hell. I wish I could live with her and Brian. He's got a Merc.'

'A what?' It sounded like some dreadful skin disease.

'Goes like the clappers too. I might go and live with them next year. I'll be seventeen then. *He* can't stop me.'

She shrugged and marched off. Then she turned and glowered at him. 'Sorry,' said Daniel, for no reason.

'You're one of those people who says sorry all the time aren't you? I can't stand it. Sorry this, sorry that. Just shut up, will you? Anyway, next year I want to leave Llanafon bloody Comp and go and live with Brian and Sheila. It's all bloody yokels that place anyway. Sheila knows this school near Reading where all these really fucked-up rich kids go; they're all on drugs, except Brian and Sheila don't know that, of course.' She chortled. 'I might get really fucked up myself and then have to come back to Hunter to be sorted out, that'd be a laugh. So why are you here then?'

It was the question Daniel had been dreading. 'Well, I . . .'

'Course, I'm not supposed to ask, but I always do. You don't half hear some stories. There was this bloke last year with a thing about black magic. We-*ird*.'

'Well, I haven't got anything like that,' Daniel said indignantly.

25

'Actually I know. You freaked out during your exams, didn't you? I read this letter on Hunter's desk. I don't care if you tell him, because then it might piss him off and he'd let me go to Sheila's. I've been working on it for years. I do all these really bad things but he just sort of smiles and forgives me. I reckon I'll have to burn the house down or something to get him really mad. Oh, Gawd, look who it isn't.'

Who wasn't it? A young man was coming down the hill and across the field towards them. He wore an ancient Norwegian sweater and filthy denims. There was something familiar about that foxy, slightly predatory face. He found a gap in the hedge and came through. 'Hi, girl.'

'Oh, it's you, Kevin,' said Dorothy rudely. 'Still buggering sheep, are you?'

'Nice girl, our Dorothy.' Kevin seemed untroubled by her. 'Afternoon.' This was to Daniel.

'Hallo,' Daniel said sulkily.

'Met you this afternoon, or my dad has, anyway. Give you a lift.'

Oh, God, so that was why he looked familiar. Surely one member of the family was enough for anyone.

'What do you think of it here? Bit exciting for you then?'

'I haven't really been here long enough,' said Daniel with dignity, 'to form an opinion.'

'Forming opinions, are you?' said Kevin with a chortle. 'I shouldn't do that. Might go blind.'

'Oh, shut up, Kevin.' Dorothy said. 'Just because *you're* thick.'

'Yes, I forgot,' said Kevin. 'We country bumpkins aren't supposed to step out of line, are we? You going to the disco Friday week, Dorothy, or is that beneath you too?'

'What, the Young Cambrians? Do me a favour. Oh, I don't know. I might, if I'm bored enough.'

'Could take you on the back of the bike.'

'*Thrills.*'

'He could come too,' Kevin said, nodding in Daniel's direction. 'More the merrier.'

'He won't be allowed,' Dorothy said bossily. 'Hunter doesn't let them do things like that.'

'Oh, doesn't he?' Kevin raised a quizzical eyebrow. 'Should have thought they could decide things for theirselves.'

'Hunter doesn't do things that way. You know perfectly well. He knows perfectly well,' she said to Daniel. 'He's only trying it on because he got into a row with Hunter last year. He was trying to get off with this girl.'

'Ugly cow,' said Kevin. 'As if I fancied her anyway. Anorexic, indeed! My arse!'

'She didn't want you, that's why you're mad.'

Kevin shrugged. 'Think I can't get myself a girl if I really want? Couldn't be bothered with that one, that was what. Look, I'll be round Friday week. Half-past seven. Look beautiful, eh?' And he was off, leaving Daniel marvelling at his technique.

'Are you going?' he couldn't help asking.

Dorothy shrugged. 'Might. Nothing else to do round here, is there? 'Sides, I ought to keep on the right side of him.'

'Why?'

'Why? It's the best thing to do with Welsh Nats, isn't it? You never know.'

'Is Kevin a Welsh Nat?'

'Well, he *says*. Just an excuse, I think really. Still, we don't want to be burned down, do we?'

Burned down! Oh, God, here was something else to worry about! How he longed for streets and supermarkets and the smell of London! The country was getting worse by the minute.

Back at the house things were not much better. For now there were three small children rushing everywhere. On being introduced to him, Rose hid her face in her skirt, Charlie asked him if he knew how to make a helicopter and when he said no, turned away without further interest, Amos giggled unstoppably and said, 'Hallo silly poo poo poo.' Oh, yes, and here came the great Celia at last, showing no signs of embarrassment, greeting him with so vague and distracted an air that he might have been transparent. Only Hunter, solid and smiling, was at all reassuring. The confusion continued with Dorothy and Celia bickering about whether or not Dorothy should tidy up the living room ('It's not *my* mess. I don't throw the bloody *Guardian* everywhere!') and the children hurling themselves around the beaten-up furniture. During this time, Joseph, wisely perhaps, was nowhere to be seen. Daniel had no alternative, once he had left his suitcase in his shabby little bedroom, but to wait in the springless armchair in the middle of it all.

Eventually, though, some kind of order was established; the children were scooped up and carried protesting up to bed and from the kitchen the clank of dishes could be heard. At home, Daniel's mother might be preparing goulash or cassoulet; the Professors ate well and copiously. Daniel felt like a prisoner starting a life sentence.

At seven thirty Celia, her face pink from exertion, called everyone to the table. From their separate corners, Joseph, Hunter and Dorothy silently emerged. The dining-room — a small dark room at the back of the house — had yellow flowered wallpaper and magenta flowered curtains. But the walls were lined to shoulder height by rich old panelling and the ancient glass in the little windows glittered in the evening sunlight.

Hunter took his place at the end of the table and smiled down embarrassingly upon Daniel. 'Welcome, Daniel, to Disserth House and our little world within a world. Usually on someone's first night we push the boat out a little, celebrate a bit and so on, but alas, the best laid plans . . . Celia had intended to cook — what was it, Celia, chicken in red wine, I believe? for your first night . . .'

'I'm so sorry,' murmured Celia.

Like hell you are, Daniel thought, but said nothing. While she ladled out the sloppy cauliflower, he thought of hot, fragrant sauerkraut, spicy noodles with poppy seed, pancakes with apple and cinnamon . . .

'I don't think Daniel likes cauliflower cheese,' said Dorothy gleefully. 'Look at his face.'

'No, I do like it, I really do,' said Daniel, who really did not.

'In Ghana,' said Joseph helpfully, 'we imagine that English cooking is all roast beef and York pudding. But this is all part of the learning experience, is it not?'

'Daniel, if you don't like it, I can always fry you an egg.'

'In a community like ours,' said Hunter, 'there has to be a certain amount of give and take, so unless someone is really allergic, or has, for example, religious objections . . .'

'Many people do not eat pork, you see Daniel,' explained Joseph unnecessarily. 'Muslims and Jews.'

'I don't blame them,' said Dorothy. 'Pork smells of smelly pigs. Yuk! I don't know how anyone can eat it.'

'I assume your objections are aesthetic rather than religious, Miss Dotty?'

'Oh, for God's sake, Joseph, do stop using such long words. And don't call me Dotty.'

'But I like to call you Dotty. It suits your character, I feel.'

'As if it wasn't bad enough being called Dorothy. I ask you, *Dorothy*!'

'What would you like to be called?' said Hunter. 'There's nothing to stop you changing your name.'

'Anything except smelly Dorothy.'

'Jennifer,' said Joseph. 'Or Pamela. Or Linda. Or Susan. I knew such a pretty English Susan once.'

'Do me a *favour*. I want an interesting name. Lara. Leonie. Scarlett.'

'Scarlet?' Joseph said. 'You would call yourself a scarlet woman?'

'No, silly, Scarlett like in *Gone With The Wind*. Lardy, lardy, Mistuh Rhett!'

'Dorothy, you're showing off now,' said Celia with unexpected venom.

'She is entertaining us,' said Hunter.

'No I wasn't,' Dorothy said, 'I was showing off.'

'This cauliflower and cheese,' Joseph put in diplomatically, 'is it a dish native to Wales? I find the study of regional cuisine most interesting. If you want to study a man, I say, look at what that man eats.'

'Or Roxanne. Or Karina. Hey, Daniel, there's this family of hippies round here and do you know what their children are called? There's Rainbow, there's Star and there's Saffron. *Yuk*! Can you imagine?'

'In Ghana,' Joseph went on inexorably, 'you are called Monday, Tuesday, Wednesday according to the day you are born. For example, for a boy born on a Monday, the name is Kwadwo, and for a girl . . .'

'I understand your mother is an archaeologist,' Celia said in her quiet way. Daniel, who had somehow not expected her to speak again, looked at her startled.

'I expect,' Hunter said, 'she would have been most interested in this house. We believe there has been a dwelling on this site since the tenth century.'

'This man called Rhodri Ddu used to have a castle here,' Dorothy put in. 'One day he invited lots of guests, got them all pissed and killed them.'

Hunter smiled pleasantly, 'Or so the story goes. The trouble is that a similar one is told about many villains of the day and there's really no reason to suppose that it's anything more than a legend. But, of course, the area round here is full of legends. And if you're here for any length of time, I hope something of that special atmosphere will begin to rub off on you. Where people have prayed and believed for many years, there's something in the air, something it's all too easy to forget in the smart twentieth century.'

'There was something in the air the other day,' Dorothy said, 'around Walter's farm. He must have been . . .' But she tailed off as her father gave her a look.

'That's why,' he went on, 'I think we've been so successful here, why, against all the rules what we do here *works*. We know that because the word has got round and we have to turn away people who have heard that it works and want to sample its atmosphere for themselves.'

This was not strictly true. Celia looked down at her empty plate with a closed expression on her face. The fact was, for the last few years they had not had to turn anyone away, quite the reverse. Ten years ago, people believed in magic and the power of men like Hunter to perform it. Now things were different; what Hunter stood for belonged with all those washed-up ideas like flower-power and universal peace. The sixties and seventies had gone forever, and of late, the nebulous ideals of Hunter's community — a kind of humanist revision of Christian ideals, where people worked in the garden and sat around a lot, talking over their problems — such ideals were less fashionable than they were. Now the community had shrunk to a trickle of people and sometimes there was nobody at all. You could cut down on the housekeeping only so much — cauliflower cheese was one of the facts of life — but after a while a point was reached. She wished Hunter would stop talking so that she could clear away and do the washing up. (*'Celia's role we see very much as a nurturing and sustaining one. She is the leaven without which we would all sink.'*)

'Would you like some more?' she said to Joseph.

'No, thank you. I feel I have experienced cauliflower cheese to the full.'

'Daniel?'

'No, thank you.'

31

'Dorothy?'

'Yuk! You must be joking!'

'Shall I clear . . .' she began, but Hunter had taken up the cue again. 'What it means for us here is that we're at the focus of a great energy source, and we simply have to find the means to plug ourselves into that source.'

'Fat lot of good it did St Rhuna,' Dorothy said. 'Look what happened to her.'

'On the contrary. Her death was added to the charge.'

'The blood of a virgin,' Joseph said. 'What symbolism we can read into that!'

'Yes,' said Dorothy. 'You would.'

'Who exactly was St Rhuna?' Daniel asked.

'I'll tell you,' Dorothy said eagerly. 'Let me tell him. She was a holy virgin right and she used to live in this cave on the hill and this Rhodri Ddu fancied her right but she wasn't having any, so one day she came down to church to pray or something and he tried to have it off with her but she said no I'm a holy virgin right and so he got mad and chopped her head off.'

'Perhaps Dorothy's choice of words is slightly different from what mine would have been, but, yes, I think that tells the story pretty clearly. There's a holy well in the church-yard which is supposed to mark the spot where she died. In fact, very soon we're hoping to hold a ceremony there to mark her saint's day, to which I certainly hope you'll be able to come, Daniel.'

'I see,' said Daniel dubiously.

'Tell you what, Hunter,' Dorothy said, 'you ought to have a real human sacrifice. All blood! Yuk! It'd be really amazing.'

'Such a thing, Dorothy,' said Joseph, 'it would not be quite cricket.' He paused, and smiled his bland, unfathomable smile. 'But then I have always found cricket to be the most horrible bore. Daniel, what do you think?'

★

Later that night, alone in his room, Daniel began a letter home. 'Greetings, O great ones,' he began, and then stopped, not really sure what he could find to say. The thing about the countryside, he thought, is that it all gets much bigger after dark. Even with the curtains closed, the blackness would not go away, but just lay there, waiting. And outside there were so many noises, everywhere small things were being painfully killed. 'Well, at last your offspring has arrived at his rural fastness. John Hunter — he likes people to call him Hunter for some reason — is a bit like Dr Ross, you know, the one when I had my poisoned finger. Mrs Hunter seems to be somewhat dopey. There is a girl called Dorothy who is a bit . . .' He crossed this out and replaced it with, 'There is also someone called Joseph something who comes from Ghana . . .'

In his room, Joseph too was writing a letter home. 'You will, I know, be pleased to hear that today I have made a new friend. His name is Lord Daniel Green and if you can imagine it, he carries around with him everywhere a battered teddy bear!'

Celia stared into the darkness. Hunter, who had long since gone to sleep, breathed evenly and heavily. A moon like a frightened white face had risen over the hill. *Wicked Celia*, said the moon. *Wicked Celia*, whispered the stars. *Wicked, wicked Celia*, cried the owl.

Chapter 3

Celia had always known that she was wicked. Other children were good, but she was a wicked child. She knew this. She thought everybody else knew it too.

Her mother died when Celia was six; this must have been her fault, she thought. She never felt close to her father; this was her fault too.

Did her teachers know how wicked Celia was? They would have described her, had you asked them, as a mousy little thing, but they did not think about her for long.

Aunt May knew, of course. Aunt May had sacrificed, as she often reminded them, her job, her prospects and her fun to look after her widowed brother and his little girl. Over the years Aunt May, who had been bright and birdlike, became wizened and hard. Little green bottles in her handbag and vivid lipstick inaccurately applied told a tale that Celia only fully understood later.

Wicked Celia! For it seemed she simply could not love Aunt May! Later, even her passionate desire to be loved by her father diminished into a kind of hopeless acceptance of his indifference. At sixteen she left school and took a job. One day her middle-aged boss tried to touch her up. When she shrank from him, he pointed out to her that she had no right to lead men on, crossing her legs in that provocative way if she did not mean business. Nevertheless, he said, he would not tell anyone how she had behaved and gratefully she worked as hard as she could for another couple of years until they made her redundant.

Her next job was as a school secretary. Here she fell in love with an English teacher as they cyclostyled programmes for the school play together in an empty classroom at night. She was grateful to him because he did not scorn her ignorance too much and she knew that he was married so, of course, there was no point getting ideas, but silly Celia, she could not help it. In her little bedsit, they made hurried love and he compiled reading lists for her.

Then, silly — or was it wicked? — Celia, got herself pregnant. She wanted to have the baby, but her lover said that was impossible for him and anyway, abortions these days were quite safe and painless. She could not understand why, if it was painless, she felt such pain. Neither could he. Really, he said, she was neurotic and he had put up with enough from her.

Celia, childless, loverless, jobless — for she could not bear to remain at the school — saw no way ahead. She bought a large bottle of aspirins and some whisky. She woke up in the hospital, a nurse bending over her. Even suicide Celia could not manage properly and the nurse left her in no doubt that with really sick people in the ward, she had been irresponsible and stupid. The suicide attempt left her in a depression. To get through every day was like trying to crawl through fog. It was at that point that someone recommended Hunter.

Ten years before, Hunter's set-up was based in a house in Buckinghamshire and it flourished. Journalists wrote about him, television men made documentaries — it was just the sort of new caring community that people felt would become the thing. There Celia went; Hunter listened to her gravely as she told her muddled, incoherent tale; he made her feel that her sins could be forgiven and she was not beyond redemption. Actually, Hunter himself was in no great shape at this stage — his second wife, Dorothy's mother, had just walked out on him and he was finding it hard to manage. (His first marriage had been a brief one years ago that he would never talk about.)

After her depression lifted, Celia stayed with Hunter. Soon they married, and they moved to Wales. Hunter told her stories in his strong resonant voice of the wonderful community they would build in the ancient, magic kingdom.

When she looked back over that time, it seemed to Celia that she was sleepwalking. By the time Amos was born, she had woken up. Rose's birth was followed by a recurrence of depression; though it lifted, it left her curiously detached from the younger children; she loved them, but not in the heart-stopping way she loved Charlie. As for Hunter, she had known for several years that she did not love him and that she was not happy. Still, she assumed that a continual vague unhappiness was to be her lot, like other people have rheumatism.

Until Jamie had entered her life.

Now there was someone who did not think she was wicked. There was no question of him tolerating her sins, as Hunter had done; he simply did not believe they even existed. Of course, she should feel wicked now; she was deep in adultery and that was the most wicked thing of all. But the weight she had carried with her for so long had lifted, and her new strength was enough to take her through all the lies. It was as though love had given her back to herself, whole and precious. What Jamie knew of her was enough to irradiate her life. Celia was good. She was a good woman.

At Disserth House that night Daniel had an erotic dream, the first one he could properly remember. Unsurprisingly, it started with Dorothy, naked in the stream. 'I always stand here, you wally,' she said in her scornful way, but then several strange and hectic things happened, with the

36

inevitable result, as he discovered the following morning, to pyjamas and sheets. It was embarrassing, but . . . yes, really rather interesting. Perhaps there would be another dream that night.

The only trouble was, that when he was dressed and trying to finish the letter to his parents, it was difficult to recapture the mood in which he had begun it. Though he tried. 'Well, quoth the rustic swain, laying down his oaten reed . . . Seriously though . . .' Seriously? There was certainly something he wanted to say but could it be said? And to his parents? 'I do feel that life here will change me, but I'm not quite sure how yet.' Here was dangerous ground and he sought for a secure foothold. 'Incidentally, we have a magic well in the village, sounds silly, doesn't it, but this bloke Hunter thinks . . .'

His parents, the Professors, married late; he was fifty, she nearly forty-one. Their students thought the whole thing ridiculous. They thought it even odder when a little later a child arrived. Shocking. Dead peculiar. But Daniel, after all, was a baby like any other and the Professors turned out to be a devoted couple, wanting only each other, Daniel and their typewriters. At breakfast in Ealing there were leisurely conversations over the Oxford marmalade. 'Have you yet read Birmgarten's chapter?' Daniel's mother, who originally came from Germany, might say. 'Does it challenge yet again the conclusions of Palmer?' To which her husband would reply, 'On the contrary, I think. The effect is rather to ratify and uphold them.' For the young Daniel, there were no bunny rabbits, no nice birdies, no pussy cats. It surprised the inhabitants of Ealing to see Daniel's mother walking rather fast in her navy mack and sensible shoes with a baby buggy, with Daniel, looking at a poster, saying, 'Why man got thing in his eye, Mummy?' To which the Professor replied, 'Ah, darling, you are looking at a picture of the battle of Hastings, in which Harold the King of England was killed by William the

37

Conqueror who had invaded England from the adjoining country of Normandy.' Daniel did not throw a temper tantrum, but solemnly asked, 'Why did Wim-er-Conkra vade Britain, Mummy?' Later, as Daniel grew up and became a teenager, Professor Green was amazed to discover that other parents considered this a tricky age. 'All this delinquency,' she said to a colleague, 'this punk, all this is most surprising to me. I cannot understand why with love and just a little firmness — yes? — it is not possible to have perfect behaviour from the young.' The colleague did not agree, but said nothing. Given time, he thought, Daniel would turn out just as unpleasant as everyone else's children. Still, Daniel passed O levels, A levels and won a place at Oxford a year early. He did not give anyone a moment's trouble. He never had done.

And then, this summer, he had taken, and not taken, his exams. Sometimes, if one thing goes wrong, it makes everything wrong that has gone before. The Professors sat up talking about it far into the night. Where had they failed? They had been good and kind, but it seemed that goodness and kindness were not enough. At the University, though some colleagues giggled uncharitably, someone else told them about John Hunter and his therapeutic community; apparently, there had been a great success with a depressed student a couple of years ago. The alternative was psychiatry and for all her briskness, Professor Green had a tender side. She knew they called this 'shrinking' and as a foreigner, found it hard to escape the literal meaning of metaphors casually used. Her delicate, sensitive son to be *shrunk*! John Hunter must cure him with kindness and country air.

And so here he was, on the first morning of that new life.

Dorothy, it appeared, was still in bed. And so was everyone else, except for the younger children, who were playing with a cardboard box in the middle of the floor. 'Hallo,' said Daniel. He knew you had to use a special voice

38

for talking to children and was pleased when Amos replied, 'Hallo, Mr Man.' Daniel decided to push his luck. 'That's a nice teddy,' he said. 'What's he called?' 'He's called,' said Amos with a pleasant smile, 'Dirty poo-poo pants.'

Daniel escaped to the armchair and tried to hide behind a three-day-old copy of the *Guardian*. Amos came up and stood by his chair, the pleasant smile still on his face. Solid and self-assured, he looked very much like Hunter. 'Do you know what you are?' he said.

'No,' Daniel replied.

'You,' said Amos gently, 'are a silly fuckie.'

Stone-faced, Daniel returned to his paper, but Amos began to dance round the room chanting, 'You're a silly fuckie! You're a silly fuckie!' Then he pinched Rose with such force that she collapsed into silent, desolate tears. Charlie, who all this time had been sitting engrossed in a book, looked up. 'Did you know,' he said, 'that a long time ago people used to think that stegosauruses had a brain inside their tails and that . . .'

'No I didn't,' said Daniel rudely, who by now had had enough of Celia's children, thus losing himself the chance of making friends with the only soulmate he might have found at Disserth House.

He went into the kitchen and found Celia.

'Goodness,' she said with a guilty smile, 'you're an early riser. I was just thinking about getting some breakfast.'

She did not look, thought Daniel, as though she was thinking any such thing, for she was drinking a cup of tea and had been staring dreamily out of the window. Around her were the remnants of last night's meal, plates and dishes still smeared with cauliflower cheese. Daniel's mother at home worked silently and with great efficiency, in conjunction with a devoted Mrs Fogg: dirty plates were washed and vanished silently into cupboards, dust sucked itself from carpets, chairs rearranged themselves, cushions swelled up nicely, clothes picked each other up and got ironed and folded away. He had never seen such a sight as this kitchen.

'Did you . . . er . . . sleep well?' enquired Celia.

He looked at her suspiciously. What was she implying? 'Yes, thank you,' he said.

'People usually do here,' Celia said. And some of them, he thought crossly, don't wake up properly.

But good manners prevailed. 'Is there anything I can do?' he said.

'Not really, thank you, Daniel. Perhaps you'd like a walk in the garden before breakfast. But, oh yes, I meant to tell you. Hunter will want to see you afterwards. At about half-past nine in his study. He'll want to brief you about your programme here. Is that all right?'

Well, it would have to be, wouldn't it? He went out into the garden and wandered there until breakfast. Dorothy still did not appear.

Which was, probably, under the circumstances, a good thing.

After breakfast, Joseph took himself for a walk in the village. St Rhuna's had one small shop, the front parlour of a cottage, which was also the post office. He had a letter to post. Behind the counter was Mrs Prothero, talking to Mrs Woosnam.

'Bore da,' said Joseph. 'Sut mae y bore yma?'

'What was that, love?'

'I was saying good morning to you.'

'Were you? Only we don't understand African, you see,' explained Mrs Prothero.

'He wasn't talking African,' said Mrs Woosnam. 'That was Welsh.'

'Welsh! We don't speak Welsh round here, I'm afraid.'

'You hear Welsh in Builth sometimes,' said Mrs Woosnam.

'Oh *Builth!*', Mrs Prothero dismissed Builth. 'Now, what can I do for you, love?'

'I'd like a first class stamp, please, if I may.'

'For here, would that be, or for Africa?'

'For here. Oxford, to be precise.'

'Don't you have any family in Africa?' Mrs Woosnam wanted to know.

'Indeed. I have a mother and three sisters.'

'Perhaps they can't read, is it?' said Mrs Prothero, consolingly.

'Oh, they can read,' Joseph said politely. 'They can read quite well.'

'Then I expect they like hearing from you.'

'I write to them every week.'

'Funny,' said Mrs Prothero. 'I don't recall selling you any stamps for Africa.'

'Perhaps Mr Hunter gets them for him in Llanafon,' suggested Mrs Woosnam.

'That's right,' Joseph said, 'I am sometimes confused with the English money.'

'Well, I can't blame you for that. I get confused myself sometimes. Just the one, is it?'

'Thank you very much, ladies,' Joseph said. As he reached the door, he heard Mrs Woosnam say, 'He's got lovely manners, hasn't he?'

He turned courteously at the door. 'N'bongo bongo bingo bong,' he said.

'What was that, love?'

'I was just saying goodbye,' he said. 'In African.'

Meanwhile, Daniel had been listening to Hunter telling him what he could expect at Disserth House. In the event, it did not seem too different from the average holiday. There was to be a bit of fruit picking, some feeding of chickens and a general reliance on what Hunter called vaguely, magic. Magic, it seemed, was to do with St Rhuna and the spirit of peace and tranquillity she had given to the village. Hunter said this as though it were a joke, but a joke to be taken seriously. 'And one final thing — if Disserth House is to work,' said Hunter, 'you have to do exactly what I say. It's an old-fashioned word, I know,' he went on, 'but I have to ask for your obedience.'

Well, this was after all what Daniel was good at. He settled down to see what demands would be made of him.

'Jamie, can I ask you to move your lovely behind?' said Deirdre. 'There . . . no, that's *marvellous*. Celia's coming round shortly to pick up some . . . so I expect we'll have a chat; you'd rather be out of the . . . two gossipy old women, not that Celia's old, *do* stay if you want, but I would have thought . . .'

'I don't mind staying,' said Jamie, casually. 'I quite like Mrs Hunter, actually.'

'Oh, dear Celia, everybody likes . . . ah look here's her car, I expect she's brought, yes she has . . . *lovely* children, of course, but poor Daddy does find them just a bit . . .'

'Who's taking my name in vain?' said Norman from the doorway. 'Ah, yes, Mrs Hunter and her brood. As you say, charming, but I think if you don't mind . . .'

'Of course not, darling, I'll send Jamie in with a cup of coffee and a . . . will you be in your study? I *hope* the flapjacks are all right, they're *supposed* to be chewy of course, but . . . Celia, *lovely* to see you, do come in. Amos, what a nice bright . . . Rose, darling, you aren't shy of Deirdre, are you?'

'Dear Celia, lovely to see you, but alas, duty calls in the form of next week's sermon. I don't suppose anyone else has any feelings on the subject of the barren fig tree, so . . .'

There was a game played at the Loftuses', trotted out for public occasions, called Happy Families. During this, Norman beamed vaguely and made scholarly jokes, the children (Jamie and an older brother and sister, now married and away from home) teased, while Deirdre fussed and bustled. Jamie did not know quite how he knew that this was somehow only a game and not how things really were, but he did. He could feel the edge of anxiety in his mother's fussings, in his father's jocularity. He hardly put this into words, even into thoughts, but it was there and it confused him.

He had had other girlfriends, but something was always wrong. Somewhere in the back of his mind he retained the memory of the perfect encounter, when Celia sat beside him and explained things with such sweet patience. Even in those days, Jamie disliked Hunter and it seemed to him monstrous that Celia should be sacrificed to him.

Not that the entire experience had been pure, for thirteen-year-old Jamie was just beginning to put together certain facts and assumptions about what the monster might do to the lovely goddess in the privacy of darkness, when Celia had leaned over his shoulder. 'No, look, Jamie, try doing it this way,' she said, though what the way was he never noticed, for her small breast brushed his shoulder and he could feel it through his shirt. Along with the flushed shame and the discomfort of trying to conceal from her the results of this sudden erotic surge, he felt a sensation of pure joy, one of those occasional moments that the mind ever after reverts to as a touchstone of what is possible. Jamie was not imaginative or discontented, he would require no more. The adult Jamie found his schoolboy crush fanned into love at his mother's table; Celia was now the whole object of his mind and body; he was quite prepared to be faithful to her for life.

As she came into the kitchen surrounded, as ever, by her brood, Deirdre's chatter fortunately filled up the huge space that would have opened between them, meeting publicly after a previous encounter so private.

'Lovely, Amos, why don't you take Rose and go and play in the . . . Charlie, dear, take Rose and Amos and go and play in the garden, give poor Mummy a rest . . . Celia, coffee or

43

tea? Now, I'm afraid the coffee's only instant, I quite forgot the other day when Jamie was in Shrewsbury and I could have asked him but it absolutely slipped my mind and you know what that stuff they sell in Spar is like or perhaps you only drink tea, do you, I know Hunter said once . . . *do* let me proffer a flapjack, though I can't say for sure that they're . . . Amos, would you like a biscuit dear? I tell you what, why not take a biscuit for you, a biscuit for Rose and a biscuit for Charlie and go and see what Tiger's up to in the . . . no, Rose, he won't scratch you dear, it was just that he doesn't like being lifted up by the . . . Celia, do sit down, next to Jamie, *poor* lamb having to listen to our gossip but he *says* he doesn't mind . . .'

'Hallo, Jamie,' said Celia stiffly.

'Hallo, Mrs Hunter.'

'And there's no need to keep Mrs Huntering the poor lady, I'm sure she won't mind if you call her Celia, will you, Celia? Jamie, *could* I just ask you to take poor Daddy a cup . . .'

Later, Jamie helped Celia carry the pile of books she had come to borrow for Hunter to the car. On the way, he whispered something in her ear that brought a dusky flush to her pale freckled face. Only Amos saw and he forgot immediately as Rose approached, anxiously trying to keep for herself a fruit gum Deirdre had given her. '*My* sweetie,' Amos said joyfully, as he snatched it from Rose.

Chapter 4

'I think,' said Hunter, 'that today would be a good day for your Quest.'

It was Monday morning. Daniel had been hoping for a quiet time in the garden reading his book and perhaps sneaking glances at a sunbathing Dorothy.

'Don't look so startled,' Hunter smiled. 'A Quest is simply our rather pretentious name for something I think you might enjoy.' He went on to explain. From what Daniel could gather a Quest was simply a long walk with an end in view. The end in his case was called St Rhuna's Cave. St Rhuna was everywhere. 'Legend has it that St Rhuna spent much time at prayer in the cave, though I believe that its holiness predates St Rhuna, perhaps by hundreds of years. It's a fascinating subject, isn't it?'

Daniel, who had just glimpsed Dorothy in a bikini passing round the side of the house, nodded mournfully.

'And all those years of holiness have charged the place with its own energy. If you go there in the right circum-stances, you'll feel that energy too. Of course, in the right circumstances doesn't mean that you bounce up there in a Ford Fiesta with four other people and a crate of lager. That's why I'm sending you up there on your own, just like the young warrior of ancient times, or the suppliant after a blessing. Go in that spirit, my boy, and I guarantee you won't come back the same person.'

None of this boded well. Apart from anything else, Daniel didn't want to be another person just yet.

'Has Joseph done a Quest?' he asked.

Ah. Joseph, it seemed, had not done a Quest. 'Between you and me, a little difficulty explaining the concept of an Ordnance Survey map. But I'm sure you have O level geography, so no problems there.'

'I see,' Daniel said. Joseph could not be relied upon to pick gooseberries, either.

'This is how we do it,' continued Hunter. 'I take you across the fields to the start of the track that goes up the hill, about half a mile away. Then I give you the map and instructions and the rest is up to you. All in all, the walk is about five miles.'

Daniel gawped.

'But I shan't ask you to walk five miles there and five miles back, never fear. If you follow the instructions, after you've seen the cave, you'll get back to the road. There's a stile and a pool there. Celia will have the car ready and she'll pick you up at one o'clock and take you to the next village for a well-earned pub lunch.'

Daniel said nothing. Hunter looked at him. 'Well?'

'It's all very well,' Daniel muttered. 'But what's the point of it?'

He expected Hunter to be cross, but instead he laughed. 'Remember, you promised obedience.'

'Yes, but . . .'

'I think you'll see the point all right when you come back this evening. But, I understand. You don't want to set off into the blue without some idea of what this bugger Hunter's got up his sleeve for you?'

'Well, I . . .'

'The point is, Daniel, once you're up there, there isn't really a way back. It's just Daniel Green, all on his own. These days none of us are on our own for long, are we? There's always someone else about, some distraction. The

46

result is that our true selves become a distant country that we never visit.'

'I see,' Daniel said, though he didn't at all.

'Jolly good,' said Hunter. 'I'll meet you by the back door in ten minutes.'

Never had the back garden seemed so immeasurably sweet as it did to Daniel now as they left it behind. The sun blazed down, almost swallowing the colours of flowers in its dazzle and releasing them in great, swooning billows of scent. Swathes of white roses scrambled voluptuously over hedges, nasturtiums were molten gold.

Hunter took him through a gate in the orchard and into a field beyond. Here was the real world and it was not very nice. Sheep stared at him with, he thought, quite definite hostility. Could you be hurt by a charging sheep?

The field sloped gently upwards. Beyond that, another field, and beyond that, a bracken slope which glowed with a deceptively gentle radiance. He was to climb the terrible red hill. At the foot of the bracken, Hunter turned and smiled. 'You're on your own now, young man. Follow the track as far as you can see and then consult these.' He handed over a pamphlet and a 1:25000 Ordnance Survey map, then he was off, striding down the field. Daniel watched him disconsolately. There was something so reassuring about Hunter, those firm brown arms, that white hair, the solid set of buttocks and hips in their beige trousers. Here was a man who would never know panic or uncertainty. 'Oh, bother,' said Daniel softly. And when he was sure that Hunter was out of earshot, he said it again, more loudly. 'Bother, bother, BOTHER.' Somewhere on a distant slope a toy Land Rover crawled vertiginously round and round. A sheep bleated, a bird squawked once, and then everything was silent again. He took the track through the bracken, towards the polished, blue sky. The ground was soft and springy, centuries of thatchy grass nibbled by centuries of sheep. Between the bracken grew patches of delicate plants,

47

little buttercups, minute speedwell, crimson leaves like miniature spears. The air was faintly blackcurrant scented, and when he turned, he found that there was nothing to be seen in any direction but hill. Even the gables and chimneys of Disserth House had vanished into the fold of the valley. He was alone on the red hill.

There was nothing else to do but keep going, up and up, fixing his eyes on the point where the track disappeared into the horizon. But when he reached the horizon, he saw that it had only been the illusion of one. Ahead of him the track still went endlessly up. He sighed, and plodded on. After some time — how the backs of his legs ached! — he approached this next horizon. But again, it proved merely a screen to the real one, which still lay in the distance. It was as though the hillside was playing tricks on him.

He decided to turn to Hunter's literature. 'Continue up the hill until the track forks and you see a dead tree.' Well, no sign of either yet. 'You are following the path that St Rhuna took when she fled up the hill to escape the evil intentions of Rhodri Ddu, or so the legend has it . . .'

In fact, there were two more of the false horizons before he came to the fork and the tree. Now, although the track still went up, the ground had flattened out considerably. 'Find your position on the map and look to your left. A marked footpath leads due west but you are to ignore this and go beyond it, where there is a far older road, visible only as a declivity in the bracken. A notch in the hill ahead will help to keep you on your path. Ancient man saw this notch, too, and made use of it.'

'Bugger ancient man!' muttered Daniel daringly, but he looked, and sure enough he could see the notch. He read on. 'Now you will have walked nearly two miles and there are only three more until you reach your goal.'

What? Three miles! Suddenly exhausted, he sat down on the grass only to find that he had sat on a pile of sheep droppings. He scrambled to his feet again brushing down his trousers. Whatever had his parents been thinking of? He would jolly well write to them tonight and tell them that he wasn't staying in this place a . . .

There was the roar of an engine, and as he watched a familiar Land Rover came into sight on the horizon, stopped suddenly and then bounced along through the bracken like a mad bull in his direction. 'Thought it was you,' said Kevin Jones. 'Want a lift?'

'The thing is, I'm supposed to be walking.'

'Walking!' said Kevin, as though the idea amazed him. 'Blimey!'

'I'm supposed to be finding this cave.'

'What, Dirty Dick's?'

'No, it's St Rhuna's.'

'Dirty Dick's is what we call the cave.'

'Oh. Perhaps there's another one.'

'Only one cave round here. It's our land, so I should know.'

'This is your land?'

'Got to belong to somebody, hasn't it? Hills is the same as any other land for a farmer. Now what's it to be, yes or no?'

Daniel calculated rapidly and made a decision. 'Yes. Please.'

'Up you get then.' And for the second time, Daniel climbed into the Joneses' smelly vehicle.

'Give us a look.' Kevin snatched the map and read. From time to time he sniggered. 'Load of old rubbish,' he said finally. 'You're not going to bother with all that, are you? He's sent you all round the houses, anyway. That bit where you're supposed to meet Mrs Hunter's only about a half-mile from here. I'll take you there if you like.'

'But Mr Hunter . . .' Daniel said helplessly.

'*But Mr Hunter!*' mocked Kevin. 'Scared of him, are you?'

'No, of course not, but . . .'

'No problem then. Go and meet Mrs Hunter straight off.

49

You don't want to waste your time at that bloody cave. Stinks of sheep's piss anyway.'

Kevin started to drive away. Daniel realized that he was being manipulated. Well, too late now. And did he really care, anyway?

'How's our friend Dorothy, then?' went on Kevin, obviously determined to do a thorough job of his corruption. 'Proper little . . . you know what I mean, isn't she?'

'What do you mean?' said Daniel unwisely.

Kevin guffawed. 'Blimey, you must be a moron.'

'No I'm not,' Daniel said. 'Anyway, I bet I've seen something you haven't.'

'What?'

'Dorothy with no clothes on.' He tried to say this in as calm a fashion as possible, but the result of it was that Kevin nearly drove into a ditch.

'*Dorothy?*'

'That's right.'

'How come?'

'She was there when I arrived. Standing in the stream with nothing on.'

There was no doubt that Kevin was impressed. 'Well, bloody hell! What did she look like?'

Daniel considered. 'She was all right.'

'I'll bet!' Kevin took his hands from the steering wheel and waved them alarmingly in the air, making a vaguely voluptuous shape. 'Was she . . .?'

'Oh, yes,' Daniel said. 'She was.'

For a while Kevin drove on in silence, with just the occasional 'bloody hell!' and 'fucking hell!' to mark his respect. Then he said, 'So what did you do, then?'

'What did I do? I went to the house, of course.'

'What, you didn't . . . you just *left* her there?'

'What did you expect me to do?'

Kevin chortled. 'Shouldn't think you needed to be told that!'

'There's such a thing as respect for women, you know,' said Daniel piously.

Kevin snorted contemptuously, but did not answer this. Soon he was deep into the subject of Perfidious Albion.

'Running all over our bloody country with your bloody holiday homes and your green bloody wellies! Think you own the bloody world don't you?'

'No I don't.'

'Rule, Britannia!' chortled Kevin. 'The bloody Queen! The bloody Royal Family! The bloody army! Eh meh ward. Jolly good show, chaps, eh? Well just you wait, bloody English, just you wait.'

'Maybe I'll get out and walk, thank you very much,' said Daniel.

'Well, you will anyway now. Look, here's the gate where you're supposed to be meeting Mrs Hunter. Sure you're all right? I can run you back if you like.' Kevin had got everything off his chest. Now he was prepared to be charming to Daniel, but Daniel was not prepared to be charming to Kevin.

'I'll get out now, thank you.'

Kevin stopped the Land Rover. 'There you go,' he said amicably. 'You'll be all right now?'

Daniel got out and watched Kevin drive off. Well, he'd avoided a long trek to the cave all right, but the only trouble was, he was far too early. Celia was due to arrive at one and it was barely eleven–thirty. This was a high bleak spot where the track joined a tarmac road beyond a gate. There was a view of distant mountains, faintly blue. He had not realized until now that the blueness of distance was anything more than a poetic fancy. Although the sun shone, the air was fresh and none too warm. A few sheep munched away, a crazed patch of dried earth marked the spot where a pool had been in winter. Something about this hill was not friendly, as though it recognized him, as Kevin had done, for the outsider he was.

Leaning against the rock within sight of the gate, he began to rehearse what he would say to Hunter. Only an hour and a half, and better than walking about a silly cave. Eleven forty-five. He tried to doze. He could hear quite clearly the hum of an insect and the distant twittering of a bird, every sound clear and distinct in the empty air. Twelve. Nothing to read, except Hunter's pamphlet. Should have brought a book. It felt quite cold now.

In the distance there was a little red car and he thought, good, Mrs Hunter's come early after all. But the car passed on and out of sight.

Twelve five, twelve ten. He tried the old children's trick of counting up to sixty; one and two and three . . . but all this did was to make one minute feel like five. He read the story of St Rhuna again, looking for bits he'd missed. There were none. He counted the trees, but gave up at seventeen. He was getting hungry. Twelve twenty-five. Twelve thirty. Thirty-five. Twenty to one. Ten to one. Nearly, nearly. Eight minutes to. Ah. Five to. Perhaps she'd be early. Go on, Celia, be early. Was that rain? Four to one, three to one, two to one and . . . Hooray. One o'clock!

One o'clock. Actually a bit past one. One past one. Two past one. Well, not really late yet. Perhaps his watch was fast. She'd be here any minute. If he counted to twenty her car would come. Or thirty. Or forty.

Five past. And it really was raining and he had no anorak.

By five past he had begun to get angry. By ten past, he had panicked.

Celia had forgotten him. Again. She'd left him stranded for a second time. And no one would notice until tea time!

Perhaps he'd got the place wrong. Perhaps Kevin had misled him.

Twenty past. Half-past. *Half-past*! He'd never find his way back. He'd starve. Freeze. Be eaten by vultures. *Were* there vultures in Wales?

Twenty-five to. Come on, Celia. Come on, *Celia*, he

said, putting as much venom into the word as possible. Come on, Cee-lee-ya. The rain was heavy now.

. And then, at nearly ten to two, there she was in her battered red car! 'I'm so sorry,' she said opening the door. Not nearly sorry enough, he thought as she smiled her vague, washed-out smile. She looked dishevelled, her shirt escaping from her waistband, her cardigan done up on the wrong button, and there was even a leaf in her hair. 'A bit of trouble with the gears, just outside Llanafon,' she went on. 'We're going to have to get something done about this car.'

'There's a leaf in your hair,' he said ungraciously. This seemed to fluster her surprisingly and she spent several minutes looking in the driving mirror, smoothing down her hair, before she would start. Ugly old thing, he thought. Who the hell cares what *she* looks like?

As they drove, she talked, more than he had ever heard her, and with a slightly nervous giggle. They discussed — or rather, she discussed, he grunted — the weather, the bad winter and how the Welsh Nationalists seemed to have got a foothold in Llanafon, while she drove erratically, lurching from side to side as they turned corners. She was not a good driver. He quite enjoyed imagining the scene in which she killed him, horribly mangled, and lived on to face the opprobrium of society.

At last they reached the pub. Look, if she thought that a sausage roll and a packet of crisps were going to make up for . . . well, nearly two hours of being kept waiting, she had another think coming. The pub was an old building recently done up. FRANK AND BRENDA MASON YOUR HOST'S WELCOME OLD FREINDS AND NEW AT THE DROVERS, said a hand-written sign below a photograph of the smiling pair. Propped up against the curly wrought iron that screened the bar, a postcard said, 'Please do not ask for credit as A PUNCH IN THE FACE often offends.'

'They're supposed to be quite a couple,' said Celia brightly. 'Why don't you try the scampi? The scampi's very nice.'

Scampi? Frank and Brenda? His parents, who always travelled expensively with the *Good Food Guide*, would not have been seen dead here. But he was hungry.

'All right.'

Brenda now appeared smiling broadly. 'And he must have a pint of our Special. All the fellows go for our Special.'

'Well, I don't really . . .'

'Oh, go on. A pint of Special. And a gin and tonic,' said Celia.

When the gin and tonic arrived, Celia drank it very fast, and to his surprise, ordered another, even before she ate her sandwich.

I bet she stopped in Llanafon for a quick one, he thought. Something wrong with the gears, indeed. I bet old Celia's on the booze. I bet soppy Celia's a bloody alkie.

Back at the house, he noticed straightaway that something was different about his room. He had tried to tidy up, just as his mother had told him, making his bed after a fashion and picking his clothes off the floor, but surely he had not left the room like this; the bed straightened with geometric precision, the brush and comb and Old Spice Shaving Foam (brought along, really, for the sake of appearance) lined up on the polished tallboy top with a little jar full of marigolds and marguerites. And there, on the bedside table, was a brightly coloured pamphlet. *Which Road To Take?* it was called, appropriately for someone who had failed to take the correct one that afternoon. On the cover, a smiling young man and woman stood on a very green hill and looked up at a very blue sky, which by some freak of weather, also contained a rainbow. 'There is only one Golden Road to Happiness!' it said, 'and it is not to be found leading you to pubs and other places of so-called pleasure!' Well, this must all be part of Hunter's plan. The Golden Road to Happiness! It had a good sound to it.

Celia, meanwhile, who was indeed not used to drinking gin and tonics before lunch and who had driven Daniel home rather faster and less carefully than she should, hurried upstairs to the bathroom, where she cleaned her teeth so thoroughly that Hunter would not guess this one at least of her secrets.

In his room, Joseph Agbodeka was writing a letter. 'The weather continues fine; perhaps this afternoon we will go for an outing on the river. I cannot tell you what a charming sight this makes — the noble colleges rising gold in the distance, the laughter of girls as they trail flowers in the water. Another fine thing that has happened is that Lord Daniel — whom I think I told you about in my last letter, has promised to take me to his family home. It is a large house, quite as big as the Broadway Hotel or the railway station and is situated somewhere in Gloucestershire. We hope to motor over the day after tomorrow. But please don't get the impression that all here is play and no work! Although so many people drop in that it can be hard to apply oneself! But now I have an essay to write, so I shall 'sport' my door as we call it and try to concentrate on the task in hand . . .' When he had finished, he read it through carefully and signed it. Then he put it into a blue airmail envelope and addressed it, 'Mrs I Agbodeka, Box No 567, Kumasi, Asante, Ghana.' He folded this blue letter neatly and enclosed it in an ordinary white envelope together with a five pound note. On this envelope he put a first class stamp and the address, 'Stephen Fowler Esq, 13 Northill Rd, Oxford.'

'Ah Daniel,' said Hunter, 'come and tell me all about your experience this morning.'

This was the bit Daniel had not been looking forward to.

55

How would he confront Hunter's questions? Then he realized that the solution was perfectly simple — all he had to do was lie! The idea had a kind of logical purity about it that pleased him greatly, although he could not remember ever having lied before. It was as though he had just uncovered some great hidden knowledge.

'So how did it go?'

'Oh, very well, sir. It went very well.'

'Daniel!'

But Hunter had only reprimanded him for saying 'sir'. And though that 'sir' must show some hidden unease, the lie itself had gone unchallenged — surely a good omen.

'And you followed my instructions all right — no trouble?'

'Oh, no trouble at all!'

'So tell me what your feelings were as you actually stood by the cave.'

Daniel considered, almost as though he were summoning up real memories. 'Well, it ponged a bit from the sheep.'

Hunter laughed. 'So it does. That's because the sheep like going there, too.'

'And it had just started to rain, and . . .'

'Yes?'

'That hill, s . . . Hunter. It's a bit peculiar, isn't it?'

'What do you mean by peculiar?'

'I don't know . . . sort of spooky.'

Hunter looked pleased. 'Ah, so you've felt it, too. But don't be frightened by it. What you call spooky is just a sign that you've responded to its power. Now, I said you wouldn't return the same person from your Quest. Was I speaking the truth?'

Just for a minute the form of words startled Daniel. Then he realized that Hunter was merely using a figure of speech. He tried to say what was required of him.

'I feel that . . . you know . . . I've achieved something. I mean it was quite a long walk . . . and hard to find . . .'

Hunter's serious nods encouraged Daniel. 'And when I got there, I felt . . .'

'Go on.'

'That I'd . . . you know . . . *got* there.'

'Good man. It sounds as though old St Rhuna didn't let you down. Anyway, I'm glad Celia met you all right.'

Hang on a minute. For surely this was the point at which to stop the tape and say, 'No, actually, she was nearly an hour late and if you ask me, she'd been . . .' But perhaps, in the circumstances, it was best to let well alone. 'Oh, yes, she met me and we went to the pub and I had scampi.'

'Good, good,' Hunter said. He was becoming distracted now as if his own more important thoughts were transporting him away.

'Oh, and s . . . Hunter?'

'Yes?'

'That book you left in my room, was I meant to read it?'

Hunter was flicking through some papers on his desk. 'Book, Daniel?'

'Yes, the road to something.'

'*The Old Straight Track*, perhaps?'

'I don't think so. Well, yes, it might have been.'

Hunter smiled, a jovial, fatherly beam. 'Well, if I left a book for you, I should say read it, don't you think, young man?'

Back in Ealing, the Professors poured themselves their evening sherry and then settled down to read Daniel's first letter from Disserth House.

'Well?' enquired Daniel's father.

'There is not very much here,' said Daniel's mother. 'His prose style — well, he is a young boy and we must forgive him. It seems Mr Hunter reminds him of Dr Ross, that Mrs Hunter cannot cook, that the weather is hot and he — seems — to enjoy himself. Really, this capacity to

57

give information that is not information, is this a feature of the young, or is he concealing things from us?'

'Give the lad a chance,' said Daniel's father with a yawn. 'Let him find his feet. After all, he's only been there a few days.'

'But the finding of the feet, how long it is to take? I wonder if we may not perhaps have done the wrong thing.'

'Give him a chance. Let him meet the others there, make friends. Time is the thing.'

'But you know, he is not like other boys of his age. I thought that this morning when I gave my first seminar. They sit around with their legs stretched out confident as old men. Daniel is not like that. He is sensitive. He worries. He does not put earrings in his ears or dye his hair blond.'

Daniel's father looked over the tops of his glasses. 'And a damn good thing too, don't you think?' He was tired, there had been a tricky meeting of the Research Committee that afternoon. Boyd–Walker had given him a hard time and he had to do a review for the next issue of PMLA. 'The boy will be all right,' he said. 'Just stop playing the anxious mother and let him get on with it.'

Daniel, meanwhile, was struggling with *The Golden Road*. 'It was such a small thing that God asked of Adam, yet even in this small thing, he could not obey and lost the chance of Paradise. Make sure that you obey, even in the smallest things . . .'

It didn't sound quite like Hunter's style, but he read it anyway.

The following morning, Daniel was awakened suddenly by the light pouring through flung open curtains. And a strange girl stood there, arrested just in the act of opening them, as surprised as he.

'Heavens!' she said, 'I thought you'd be up. You missed breakfast, you know.'

58

He pulled himself up amid the sheets and stared at her through bleary eyes. 'Nobody called me,' he said crossly.

The girl laughed, brightly. 'They don't *call* you here, you know!'

'People usually knock before they come in, though.'

'So they do. And so I did, but you were deaf to the world. You must be Daniel. I'm Anita.'

She was a pretty girl, fresh-faced, with a soft, peach-like bloom, forget-me-not blue eyes, a little *retroussé* nose and a mass of fine, light brown curls. Her little white teeth seemed expressly designed to bite into apples. Her skirt was patterned with white daisies on a pale green ground, she wore a white blouse with a lace collar and a cardigan of palest, softest green. He had never before met anyone whose appearance spoke so eloquently of fresh air and healthiness.

'Well, since I'm here,' she said, 'I may as well dash round with the Hoover. I can do the bed later on when it doesn't have you in it.'

'Hoover?'

'Yes, I'm *Anita*,' she said, as though it explained everything. 'Didn't they tell you?'

'I didn't know there was anyone else in the house at the moment.'

'Oh, I don't *live* here!' she said, as though he had said something hugely amusing. 'I live in Llanafon. I come in on the dreaded motorbike three days a week. Don't tell me you haven't seen the dreaded motorbike.'

No, he hadn't. But there was obviously much he didn't know.

'Block your ears!' she cried gaily. 'I won't be a tick!' and the Hoover roared into life. She was very quick, but he would not have minded if she had taken longer; she was so nice to watch in her flower-spangled skirt. Then she switched off the Hoover, straightened up and smiled at him. 'There now, that wasn't too bad, was it? Now I'm just off to do Mr and Mrs Hunter's room, which will give you time to make yourself respectable before I come back.'

'Just a minute!' he called, though he really had nothing to say.

'What is it, Daniel?' How seldom people used your name when they spoke to you, but how comforting it could be! Suddenly he remembered something that he did want to ask her.

'Was it you left that pamphlet here the other day?'

She laughed, showing her little teeth like a pearl necklace. 'Oh dear! Now you'll get me into hot water with Mr H! I just popped it under — what was that book you were reading? Goodness, it looked terribly deep.'

'Not really, it's by George Eliot, it was . . .'

'Well, it *looked* deep to me,' she said, cutting him off. 'Mind, I like a good read myself, but you can't often find one these days, unless you enjoy pornography, which, quite frankly, Daniel, I don't.' Taking a bright yellow duster out of her pocket, she gave his window-sill a quick flick. 'So what did you think of my little book, may I ask, Daniel?'

'Do you always go round leaving things for people to read?'

She put her duster down and looked serious, standing with her hand on her hip. 'Put it this way, Daniel. What do you do when you've had some very good news? Do you keep quiet about it, or do you rush off to tell someone?'

'Tell someone, I suppose.'

'Exactly! Still, I mustn't stand around gossiping, I've got work to do! But if you enjoyed my little book, I'll leave you another one. I've got one that I think might really appeal to someone clever like you. All right?'

'Oh, yes. Yes, it is.'

'And the next time I come we must find time for a little chat. How about that?'

'Oh, yes,' he said. 'Yes.'

Chapter 5

'Our car rolled along through magnificent English countryside, past fields of waving golden corn and meadows
where placid cows grazed on the rich grass. Bent old men
with wrinkled ruddy faces came out of the pub and waved
as we passed. Bless you, my lord! they cried. Soon a pair of
magnificent gates greeted us with a long drive stretching
beyond. At the end of the drive, stood an ancient pile . . .'

Joseph paused. He imagined his readers being puzzled by
this. An ancient pile of what? So he altered it to 'a stately
mansion'. Then, dazzled by his powers, he continued, 'The
car came to a halt on the sweeping gravelled drive. A flight
of broad steps led up to a splendid portal whereon waited an
elderly retainer in a suit of tails. Eagerly he rushed to greet
us . . .' Would an elderly retainer rush? A writer had to
think of such things. He altered 'rushed' to 'hobbled' and
hoped his tone was not becoming too sycophantic. He
wrote, 'Mason, as the old butler is called, has known
nothing but a life of feudal service, as has Mrs Fortnum, the
housekeeper, but the Earl is a kindly man and treats his
people with fatherly concern . . .'

Joseph sighed and put down his pen. Outside innocent
puffs of cloud gathered like baby lambs in a sky of tender
blue. 'I am a bad man,' he said to the sky, and for a moment,
sank his head on his hands in deep dejection. But this
thought was soon succeeded by another which had the

effect of cheering him up. 'A *good* bad man nevertheless,' he said, and he returned his attentions to the Earl's welcome.

'Jamie, darling Jamie . . .'

'Quickly, inside so no one sees. How long have we got?'

'Only about half an hour. I'm supposed to be collecting some wire for the chicken run. I've left the car just in that dip by the ruined house. What about you?'

'Oh, I told Ma I'd be bird-spotting in the woods. Bird-spotting! Celia-spotting, Beautiful-lovely-Celia-spotting. How long did you say?'

'Half an hour. Just.'

'Half an hour,' he said unbuttoning her blouse. 'Thirty minutes. One thousand eight hundred . . . oh, Celia . . . seconds. I shan't waste any of them. God, your breasts are delicious. Celia, I've missed you so much you've no idea . . .'

Sex had never been like this before. With her school-teacher lover every act was an O level examination. ('Shall I do it this way? Or this? For God's sake, woman, of course you know!') For Hunter it was a ritual of physical and mental hygiene necessary for the smooth running of the great machine of his ego.

Sometimes the age difference meant that there were times when Jamie seemed like her son; certainly she felt some-times that she was embracing some perfect adult version of Charlie, with all his innocent beauty; at other times, he could be like an older brother, teasing and protective.

'What are you thinking?'

'Oh . . . I love you. Just that.'

'Yes, you can go on thinking that, as long as you like . . . No, it isn't only that, is it?'

'Oh, you know . . . Hunter.'

'Hunter,' he said bitterly. 'I might have known we couldn't get away from Hunter for long.'

'Sorry. But I feel guilty.'

'Why the hell should you feel guilty? On *his* account?'

'He is my husband, Jamie.'

'I was actually aware of that.'

'And having to lie . . . things like that.'

'Lying isn't the worst thing there is. Being a bastard is. Having a lovely wonderful thing like you and treating you like dirt is.'

'Jamie, he doesn't really . . .'

'Doesn't really what?'

'Treat me like dirt. Not really.'

'He does. You know he does.'

'He means well.'

'Yeah, like a boa constrictor means well. Celia, shut up about Hunter, will you? Why must you always try to see the good side of people? Some people don't have a . . . God, you smell wonderful, did you know that? I want to eat you . . .'

'But we'll have to think about Hunter soon, won't we? I mean we can't go on like this for ever.'

'I can go on like this for ever. Oh, damn.' Jamie raised himself up on to his elbows and started to button up his shirt. 'He always wins, doesn't he? Even when he's not here.'

'I'm sorry . . .'

'Celia, tell me just one thing.'

'What?'

'You do love me, don't you?'

'You know I do, but . . .'

'But what?'

'But everything.'

'But nothing. And you know I love you?'

'Of course, but . . .'

'So what are you worrying about, stupid woman? I love you. You love me. I know it, you know it. And we'll do something about it.'

'What *can* we do?'

'What the hell do you think? Get married.'

'Do you want to be married to me?'

'What else do you think I want?'

'But . . . married.'

'I don't see the problem.'

'I do. He's called . . .'

'Yes, I know, I know,' he said wearily. 'Do me a favour, just don't say his name, right? Just let's keep him out of the picture for five minutes.'

'I don't see how I can. I'm married to him.'

'You hate him.'

'Yes, but . . .'

'No problem. Divorce him.'

'How can I?'

'That's what lawyers are for, Celia my love. So that people can stop being married to bastards they don't love and get married to bastards they do.'

'It's not as easy as that.'

'Why not?'

'Well . . . the children . . .'

'What about the children?'

'Jamie, be sensible. I can't just leave them.'

'You won't have to.'

'What are you talking about?'

'The children. Bring them with us.'

'With us where?'

'Where we go, of course.'

'But where can we go?'

'Somewhere. Anywhere. Don't worry.'

'Jamie, this is fantasy.'

'It isn't fantasy. I've been thinking of nothing else for days. We'll go away together somewhere; London probably. We'll find a flat and I'll get a job. Then, hey presto, it's goodbye to Bluebeard.'

'With the children?'

'Of course. They're your children. If you want them, I want them.'

64

'They're also his children.'

'He can't actually stop you taking them. This isn't the nineteenth century, remember.'

'You don't know him. You don't know how he does things.' Celia remembered, but did not tell Jamie, how Dorothy's mother used to ring up in tears, begging to be allowed to see Dorothy, and how Hunter always found a way to refuse.

But for the next few moments, it was almost possible to believe in what Jamie had said. It was simple. They loved each other. They could make it happen.

She thought about it later on as she drove home in the car.

They loved each other all right. But — and maybe it was the real difference between twenty-two and thirty-three — she knew that nothing in this world was simple; not even love. Especially not love.

When she returned to Disserth House she had been away no more than an hour and a half, but being with Jamie always made the return home seem like a journey through light years. This was her dangerous time, adjusting to the everyday world again; the time when Hunter might accuse her of acting strangely, or Dorothy draw loud attention to some change in her behaviour. But today, Hunter had just received a telephone call from Woman's Hour; some years before they had interviewed him for an item on alternative life-styles, and now they wanted to do a follow-up, perhaps using his well ceremony as a focus. Honoured, recognized, Hunter was glossy with self-satisfaction.

The children were in the living-room, drawing pictures to illustrate the story Anita had just read them. As usual, they were engrossed; Anita seemed to exert some magic spell. Celia did not mind this; those sorts of jealousies were not part of her nature, but she did resent the creamy smile with which Anita said, 'They've been so good; they never give me any trouble. But now if you'll excuse me, I must get on. I have to do the kitchen floor yet.'

'That's all right,' said Celia helplessly. 'You won't have time now and I don't like you running late.'

Anita's smile stretched a millimetre further and her blue eyes were hard as sapphires. 'You know me, Mrs Hunter, I'm not a clock watcher.'

'Mummy, Mummy,' said Amos. 'I done a wilf, look at my wilf.'

'Not a wilf, stupid,' interposed Charlie. 'It's a wolf.'

Rose giggled. 'He say I huffipuffi BLOW your house down.'

'And the pig said Mummy the pig said Oh no you don't you stupid wilf.'

'*Wolf*.'

'So 'e huff an' puff . . .'

Anita waited at the door for the compliment which Celia knew in all justice she could not withhold. 'You're so good with them, Anita.'

'I *love* children, Mrs Hunter. You know that.'

Well, probably she could have done worse than the three little pigs. Last week it had been Moses and the Plagues of Egypt in all their gruesome details; for while tender-hearted Celia bowdlerized her stories so that grannies and ginger-bread men did not get eaten, red shoes were not cut from feet, giants not skewered through the eye, Anita had no such compunctions and retained all the primitive horrors. Which, of course, the children loved.

Celia watched them as they bent over their drawings; Amos solidly squatting, the crayon firmly clasped in his short fingers; he would take as firm a grip on his life, making it fit his requirements. Rose, on the other hand, the child of depression, seemed set to become one of life's victims, prone to floods of tears, plaintive, put upon. Was Rose doomed to be a carbon copy of her mother? Only Charlie, with his serious composure, his transparency and

imagination, seemed to take only after himself, and sometimes she loved him so much it was painful. Now she
remembered how she had almost, briefly, forgotten them
as she made love to Jamie. The memory so filled her with
shame that she picked Rose up and held her close. But Rose,
who had been enjoying herself on the floor, wriggled away,
and perhaps sensing on her the smell of Jamie, said, 'Go
away, Mummy; you smell like a different Mummy today.'

At breakfast the following morning Daniel stared at his
piece of toast. What he really wanted to stare at was
Dorothy, who was looking rather good this morning in a
white sleeveless thing and a minute skirt. But that night he
had had another dream in which Dorothy figured, and it
was present so vividly in his consciousness that it was
awkward to have the real Dorothy so close.

However, his embarrassment did not last long. Dorothy
was off to see a friend and go swimming in Llanafon. She
left the table with a flounce of blonde hair. Daniel watched
her go with mixed feelings. She returned briefly, but only
to fling a bundle of letters on the table. The letters showered
down before Hunter, who picked them up as of right.
'Joseph. Looks like a letter from home. Daniel, ditto. Bills,
bills, bills for me, of course. Joseph, another. You are
popular today. Mr and Mrs Hunter. Celia, perhaps you'll
open that. And another; that writing looks familiar. More
bills, I have no doubt. *The Time–Life Book Of Endangered
Species.* Hmm. Ah, this looks like my girlfriend at
Woman's Hour, bless her. It seems that we might get quite
a bit of publicity for dear old St Rhuna . . . Celia, open your
letters. Why are you dreaming?'
'Excuse me please,' said Joseph. 'I shall take my letters
upstairs.'
'Er — yes, I'll be off too,' said Daniel. Amos grabbed a
wet handful of Honey Puffs from his sister's plate and she
screamed. At the same time, Charlie, who had been sitting

engrossed in a book on dinosaurs, took the opportunity to deliver a lecture. 'Mummy, did you know that reptiles can't fight for very long because their blood's cold and they get tired, but mammals, Mummy, can fight for a long time, so if a dinosaur and a mammal have a fight . . .'

Celia stared at her letters with shaking hands and a sudden dry mouth. Certainly that writing was familiar . . .

'Celia?' said Hunter. She picked up the other letter, to put off the awful moment. Hunter watched while she read it. It was short and to the point, from the mother of a girl who was supposed to be arriving at Disserth House the following week. It seemed that the girl had gone back on to heroin and vanished with her boyfriend. The mother was sorry, but she had no alternative but to cancel the booking.

Hunter despatched the problem quickly but crossly. 'You'll have to write to the mother and insist on a week's fee at least. Tell her we've had to reserve a place, turn down other people, that sort of thing.'

'But we haven't,' Celia said.

'Darling, I know that, but they don't. Be a good girl and do what I say. Now, who is the other one from?'

It could be put off no longer. Celia's face was the colour of Amos's milk as she opened it. But the letter was short, polite and quite uncompromising.

Dear Mr and Mrs Hunter,
When I was in Hay the other day, I managed to find some stuff that might interest you. There's a very good piece on well-dressing in a book by Dr Aneirin Griffiths written in 1850, and a *Life of St Teilo* in a 1918 reprint. I could bring them round to church next time there's a service, or perhaps you or Mrs Hunter might like to pop round.
                    Yours sincerely,
                    James Loftus

Celia's hand was still trembling as she held it out to Hunter. 'Nice of him,' said Hunter. 'He's a good lad, that one. Perhaps you could find time to call at the vicarage this morning, Celia? It's one of Anita's days, isn't it?'

Daringly, Celia replied, 'I'm a bit rushed today. Why don't you go?'

But she knew what Hunter would answer, and he did. 'Not a chance, my love. I've got a mountain of paper work to do this morning. Besides, you'd like the chance of a gossip with Deirdre.'

Who would not be there, Celia remembered. She and Norman were spending a few days with their married daughter in Wolverhampton. Clever Jamie, she thought. Clever, beautiful Jamie . . .

Daniel's letter was from his mother. '. . .so pleased to hear from you, my darling, but we long to know more. How does this Mr Hunter's regime work? It sounds as though perhaps he is a Jungian; what do you think? And does he get you to talk about yourself? I feel it is necessary for you to talk about what happened this summer in order to overcome it. Daddy and I as you can imagine have been talking too. The question we ask ourselves is have we perhaps been too hard on you and expected too much? Because you complain so little perhaps we have assumed too lightly that we have been doing the right thing when all the time the opposite is the case. Not everyone in this world is cut out for University; there are plenty of other things to do. Only please, my darling, let us hear from you, let us know what you are thinking . . .'

Daniel put this aside in some impatience. What on earth was she on about? All she could think about was university. Typical.

Joseph was in his room too. When he left the dining room, it had been with a cheerful smile, but now the smile had left his face. He, too, had dreamed last night but it had been an anxiety dream in which he had waded helplessly through mud on his way to some vital appointment. He needed no help to interpret the meaning of that. All around him were signs of unfinished business. There was *Teach Yourself Chartered Accountancy*, *Teach Yourself Management*, *The Penguin Guide To English Literature: vol 2*, *Teach Yourself Welsh*. All had been looked at, none mastered. The road to Hell, thought Joseph, is paved with Teach Yourself books.

His first letter was from his sister Elizabeth. 'Mother asks me to write how proud we all are here at number 173! How well you are doing at Oxford, and we are not surprised that so many rich and aristocratic people want to meet you. But you must not let the excitement run away with you! The important thing after all is your studies; how we long to see your photograph in that precious gown! Well Joseph after all the excitement you will find our life here very dull — though I must tell you that business continues well and we are hoping to open another store next year in Station Road — it continues difficult to get stock, but Mother as always is amazing and can conjure things out of the thin air! It seems that everyone wants to shop at Independence Stores! As for the rest of us, Mary hopes that next year she will be made Matron, and Prudence has just passed with 'flying colours' a visit from the schools inspectors — I think Yaa Asantwaa Junior is really the best school in Kumasi . . .'

His second letter was a depressing reminder of how low he had sunk:

Dear Joe,
How's tricks with you old man? I hope life is treating you better than it is me at the moment, I am getting all sorts of hassles here, I can tell you. Actually, that's why I'm writing; they were round here the other day asking where you were, and a fiver doesn't go anywhere these days and it just isn't worth the hassle. Of course I

wouldn't tell them where you are and all that, but you can't expect me to take risks for you and sending on your letters is getting to be a risk believe me. Make it twenty and maybe I won't tell them. All the best,

Steve

It took Joseph some time to understand all the implications of this note. When he did, they were not very nice. I am being blackmailed. Steve is blackmailing me. Though, he thought, taking into account the colour of Steve's complexion and doubtless that of his liver, too, perhaps *whitemailed* would be a more appropriate term.

But where to find twenty pounds? How to continue finding it? And what did they do to you when they caught you outstaying the fairly scanty hospitality afforded to an alien on British soil?

It was all too much. Joseph buried his head in his hands.

Chapter 6

Daniel's task the following morning was to scythe the thistles in the top field. This sounded easier than it was; there were so many thistles and the scythe left blisters on the palm of his hand. Moreover, he couldn't suppress the mutinous thought that the work was doing more for Hunter's husbandry than for his own soul.

Over the hedge he caught a glimpse of Kevin. 'Morning, Kevin!' he called out.

But he was not to know that Kevin was in a foul mood. Kevin had just spoken to Dorothy who had breezily informed him that she was not going to the disco with him after all. Having boasted to all his mates that he was bringing this bird who was really something, he would now have to go shamefully on his own.

'Oh, it's you,' he snarled at Daniel.

'How are you?'

'Bloody English parasite!'

'Hey,' said Daniel, mildly shocked. 'No need for that.'

'No need for you either,' said Kevin nastily. 'No need for any of you. Well, just you wait and see, that's all!'

'Are you threatening me?' Daniel said in surprise.

Kevin gave a smile like a row of knives. 'You'll just have to wait and see about that,' he said.

'You're just a loudmouth,' Daniel said. 'I don't believe you could do anything.'

'Oh, don't you? Then that just shows what a fool you are, don't it? Well, like I said, you just wait and see. And you won't have to wait too long, I'm telling you!'

Kevin did not believe in people who made threats without carrying them out. Damn, he thought to himself as he marched away across the hill, that's torn it. Still, they're all bloody snobs, the lot of them. They deserve it, whatever it is.

Slightly shaken, Daniel returned to the house. Hunter was in his study, on the phone. 'That's right, Disserth. That's d-i-double s . . . yes, it's an old Welsh word meaning a hermitage, a wilderness, the same as the English desert actually . . . Look, not just now, there's a good boy, Daniel. Yes, thirteenth century at least, but quite possibly older . . .'

Well, thank you very much, thought Daniel. Easy to see where John Hunter's priorities lay! But in the living-room was Anita, standing behind a pile of ironing. Today she wore a cotton top and trousers of purest palest yellow with a primrose ribbon gathering her soft curls together. Moreover, unlike just about everyone else he had encountered that morning, she seemed pleased to see him.

'Actually,' he said, 'I've just had rather an unpleasant experience,' and he told her about Kevin.

At once she was all concern. 'Oh, poor you! Shall we have a coffee? It's time for my elevenses. I'm afraid manners round here aren't always all they should be. Milk and sugar?'

When she returned with the coffee, he was very happy to continue with the subject. 'I mean it's not just Kevin, it's . . . oh, Mr Hunter's always busy and that Celia looks half asleep and the children use bad language, and Dorothy . . . Dorothy . . .'

Anita nodded. 'Say no more, Daniel.'

Encouraged, he went on in a burst. 'I mean it's not as though I *want* to be here, is it, but you'd think they'd try a bit harder.'

'Still, Mr Hunter's wonderful,' Anita said. 'He works so hard doesn't he, keeping this place together, but he can't do it single-handed and quite frankly, Daniel, though I know I shouldn't be saying this, but we *are* friends, I don't think he gets altogether enough support from we-know-who.' Anita took up her iron again and began to spray steam on a pile of shirts. The iron puffed and hissed like a dragon.

He wasn't quite sure he did know who, but fortunately, her next words explained it. 'If a wife doesn't hold the house together, then who will?'

Daniel was very glad to join in this one. 'Oh, Celia! Yes, do you know, when I arrived she'd forgotten to meet me at the station? I had to get a lift from some smelly farmer.'

Anita lowered her voice. 'There are quite a few things our Mrs Hunter forgets, I'm afraid. Like her children's manners, for example. Mind, it's not the kiddies' fault is it? They only repeat what they hear other people say.'

'*I* certainly never used language like that when I was little.'

'Goodness, no! I don't think I even *knew* those words. But then I had a very loving caring mother, Daniel, and I expect you did too.'

'And Dorothy,' Daniel said daringly. 'I really think someone needs to take Dorothy in hand.' The prospect of someone — him? — doing this was quite exciting.

Anita put down her iron. 'Dorothy, I'm afraid, is a flirt. Still, I'm sure she'll be given her reward. Now then, Daniel, what about the little book I left you the other day? Have you had time to have a think about it?'

Well, not really. His mind was full of other things, but this, of course, he could not say to Anita.

'I knew you'd enjoy it,' said Anita. 'It is a nice one, isn't it, *Your Debts Paid In Full*. I'm very fond of it.'

Daniel felt the habits of his expensive education tugging him away from too facile an agreement. 'But the thing is, Anita, all that stuff, the Bible and all that, you can't take it literally, can you?'

But Anita had obviously been here before. '*Can't* you, Daniel? Give me an example of something you find hard to take literally.'

'Well, about God making the world in seven days and the garden of Eden and that. The apple tree.'

She smiled at him across the ironing board. 'Well now, Daniel, for a start, when we talk about a day, we're talking about one of God's days. A day for God is like a thousand years to us. Now you aren't telling me that *God* couldn't have made the world in *seven thousand years*, because that's what we're talking about, isn't it?'

'I suppose so, but . . .'

'And what makes you so sure it was an apple tree, Mr Clever? You just go back and read Genesis chapter one again. Now it makes no mention of an apple tree, does it?'

'Well, that's another thing,' said Daniel. 'All that stuff about God not letting them eat the apple. Or whatever it was. What was so bad about that?'

'God told Adam and Eve not to eat it,' said Anita mildly.

'But when someone tells you not to do something, you want to do it all the more, don't you? I mean it's human nature.'

Anita considered. 'Well, it's *fallen* human nature, certainly.'

'But they just wanted to try it, that's all.'

'And you think God should have let them, do you?'

'Yes, I do.'

'I see. And if your little boy wanted to drink a bottle of bleach, would you let him?'

'No, of course not. But . . .'

'Or stick his fingers in an electric socket?'

'No, but . . .'

'Well, there you are! After all God's our father, isn't he? He just does what any father does for his children.'

'So you really believe every word in the Bible, do you?'

'Every word, Daniel. Why shouldn't I?'

75

For a moment, Daniel heard the voice of his mother hanging in the air. But smiling Anita was every bit as confident and, moreover, she was *there*. 'I know what you're trying to say, Daniel, that the Bible is just a collection of fairy-tales, aren't you?'

'I'm sorry, Anita, I'm not trying to be rude.'

'Oh, don't be sorry. I'm used to it. Those of us who follow God's Law are very much in the minority these days, I'm afraid. But we don't really worry because we know that on the Last Day, God will reward us.'

'And what will he do to all those other people?'

Anita looked serious. 'It doesn't give me any pleasure to think about that, Daniel. But I'm afraid there are no two ways about it; the people who chose to ignore God's law will go to . . .'

The iron gave a despairing gasp and the word seemed to hover nastily in the air between them. Bravely, Daniel tried to articulate it.

'Do you mean . . . *Hell*, do you mean?'

'It's not a nice thing to think about, is it?'

'But what about all the people who believe other things, like Buddhists?'

Anita picked up a T-shirt.

'What colour is this, Daniel?'

'Yellow, but . . .'

'It's not green, or blue, is it? You're quite sure about that, aren't you? Because you see there can only be one truth. A thing either *is* true, or it *isn't*.'

'It seems a bit unfair on the Buddhists,' muttered Daniel.

'Well, we brought it all on ourselves, didn't we? Now you see why what Adam did in the garden was so bad.'

There still might have been a chance to save world Buddhism, but at that moment Hunter put his head round the door and the chance was gone. 'Just off to catch the post. Hold the fort, will you?'

76

He had been gone only a few moments when the phone rang in his study. Daniel looked doubtful. 'I suppose I'd better go.'

Anita laughed. 'It won't *bite* you, Daniel.'

Daniel was not too sure about that. What mad person might not be on the line? But the man's voice at the other end, asking for Mrs Hunter, seemed quiet and rather hesitant. Daniel replied that she had gone to Llanafon.

'It's James Loftus here. I don't think we've met. It's just that . . . Mrs Hunter asked me the other day where she could get . . . ah . . . some Jacob's wool. I just phoned to say that I know this man near Builth who has some.'

'Jacob?' Daniel was confused. 'Wool?'

'It's a breed of sheep. They have brown and grey wool.' The voice at the end of the line was curiously toneless.

'All right, I'll tell Mrs Hunter. Man outside Builth. Jacob's wool.'

'I'm going that way tomorrow. I could get her some, you see. Mr Hunter's out, is he?'

'He's just gone to the post. Shall I tell him you called?'

'Oh, no . . . that is, it's not important. If you could just tell Ce — Mrs Hunter.'

'Yes,' said Daniel, as he put the phone down. After so straightforward a call, he could not say why he should feel puzzled, but he did. 'That was someone called Loftus, with a message for soppy Celia,' he said, and blushed, not having meant to let slip his private nickname for her. But Anita merely giggled.

'He's the vicar's son, I think, isn't he? So what did he want?'

'Something about this wool. Jacob's, I think.'

'Yes, Jacob's wool, yes, that's right, go on.'

'Well, that was it, really. She wants to make a sweater and he knows where to get Jacob's wool.'

'Oh, I'm knitting the loveliest sweater, the most gorgeous pink, really pale and fluffy. Of course, you don't want

77

to be vain, do you, but on the other hand, I think you owe it to other people to look as nice as you can.' She stopped suddenly. 'Did you say knitting? Mrs *Hunter*?'

'That's right.'

'Well, how very peculiar. I was talking to Mrs Hunter only the other day, in fact I was telling her about my lovely pink sweater, just like I told you today, and she said she *never* knitted, couldn't bear knitting in fact. She was rather rude about it, I thought. And now you say she wants some Jacob's wool to make a sweater. Now that *is* odd, don't you think?'

Chapter 7

'Daniel,' said Anita, 'I've just had a little thought.'

It was later that same morning. Anita, astride her motorbike — the dreaded motorbike — was ready to go. Even in a crash helmet she looked fetching, and mounted on the machine, a few fair curls escaping at her neck, she was like a Nordic princess clad for battle, in a land where castles perched, glittering in the golden mists of morning. 'Why don't you,' she continued, 'come to our service on Sunday?'

'Service?'

'We have a lovely Meeting House, in Llanafon. Really Daniel, you'd love it, and we're packed out for Morning *and* Evening service. Do come!'

'But I . . .'

'Oh, it's great fun, and afterwards you can have lunch at the Community House and meet the Saints.'

'Saints?' he said in horror.

She laughed prettily. 'Really it just means those who obey God's Law and that's us.'

But the thought of meeting saints had taken him aback. 'I really don't know. You see, I'd have to ask Hunter. He . . .'

'Mr Hunter? How can he mind? You're a free agent, aren't you?'

Was he? Was anybody? 'Well, not really, Anita, you see . . .'

'You're not telling me that Mr Hunter is going to stop you going to the Lord's service, on the Lord's day, are you? Didn't you tell me earlier that you wanted to find out what it was all about? Remember, we had such a nice little talk. You said you thought there was a lot of sense in it all.'

Daniel searched in his recent memory. He could not recall this quite as clearly as Anita, but if she said so . . . Yes, of course. In fact, now he came to think of it, he was . . . quite . . . well, almost very sure that there had been a nice little talk. 'Oh yes, but . . .'

She gave him a sly look. 'Daniel, you haven't been listening to all those silly stories about *brainwashing* have you? Because I can assure you nothing like that goes on with us! As if we need to brainwash!'

Daniel still paused uncertainly.

'Oh, Daniel,' she said, in quite a different voice, 'you don't make it easy for a girl, do you?'

Good Lord! Was she blushing? Well, what else could he say after that but, 'If I come, how would I get there?'

'Easy!' she said in her normal voice. 'I'll pick you up on the dreaded motorbike. Ten thirty?'

'Yes. Great.'

'Daniel, you've made my day, I can't tell you. Cheerio then, till Sunday.'

'Cheerio,' he said happily. 'Cheerio.'

For that evening, Hunter had promised what he described as 'another of our little Disserth rituals'. He hinted at 'interface with the community' and 'bridge building'. Dorothy said crossly later, when Daniel asked, 'Oh, it's just a glorified poetry reading. Dead boring.'

The other person to snap at him that afternoon was soppy Celia. Well, it was hardly his fault that at first he'd forgotten to give the message about the Jacob's wool. It didn't seem to be really important, and so it slipped his mind till about half-past five. Celia went into a flap that managed to be both waspish and vague. 'I really must ask you to pass on messages in future. He'll think it very rude of me.'

Anita was right. There was something most peculiar about all this.

Dorothy, as it happened, had other things on her mind too. She changed into a minuscule striped green and white skirt and a scanty vest. Then she went into Joseph's room to find him hastily pushing something under a pile of papers. 'You are looking guilty. Are you doing something bad?'

'Not at all. I am simply writing a letter home.'

'You didn't half jump when I came in.'

'This expression has always troubled me,' he said, recovering his composure. 'Does it mean that I did not jump? Or that I made only a half jump, or something that was neither one nor the other? Enlighten me, please.'

'Joseph, shut up,' said Dorothy wearily. She sauntered into the middle of the room and threw a casual glance in the direction of the desk at which Joseph was writing. Meanwhile, he pushed the letter even further under his copy of the *Mid-Wales Monitor*. (In fact, Dorothy could have seen it without suspicion. He had written, 'Well, you may be surprised to receive a letter from me with this postmark. Have you ever heard of Wales? It is a charming little country just to the left of England and I am staying at present in a delightful house belonging to friends.')

Dorothy placed herself in front of him, with her hands firmly on her hips. There was an expression of solemn determination about her. 'Joseph, I want to ask you something.'

'Now, the correct expression for that is, You are my guest. No, wait a minute. Be my guest. Yes, that's it. Please be my guest, Dorothy.'

'No, seriously, listen.'

'Yes, seriously, I listen. Please ask.'

'Well, look. I want you to seduce me.'

81

Joseph's mouth fell open. He was silent for a few minutes, then he said, 'Dorothy? I'm not sure I heard you correctly.'

'You heard me.'

'Yes,' said Joseph, 'so I feared.' He rose and walked over to the window. 'Then, may I ask, Dorothy, why you want such a thing?'

Dorothy tossed her head. 'God! That's obvious, isn't it, I should have thought.'

'Not to me.'

'Well, look at me! I'm sixteen and I'm still a virgin.'

'In some circles this might be counted an advantage.'

'Oh, come *on*, Joseph!'

'You are still a child, Dorothy.'

'A child!' she said in amazement. 'I'm *ancient*! Most people have had their first *abortion* by now!'

'Is it so?' he said humbly. 'I was not aware of this.'

'Well, then, will you do it?'

'Will I what, Miss Dorothy?'

'Oh, for heaven's sake, how thick can you get?'

'Dorothy, I am in your father's house.'

'So what?'

'Now it's you who are being . . . thick.'

'I can't see why all the fuss.'

'You seem to think this is a simple thing that you ask. I assure you it is not.'

'Perhaps you don't fancy me.'

'Oh, no, Dorothy, that is not the reason.'

'Perhaps you're imp . . . imp . . . whatever they call it.'

'Most certainly not!' he said indignantly.

'Then why are you looking at me like I'm something the cat brought in? I'm offering you something nice, at least it's supposed to be nice, I wouldn't know, and you're being all indignant.'

Joseph tried again. 'Listen, Dorothy, what you are saying is on . . . one level . . . most tempting. But there are things that make it impossible. For one thing, it is an abuse of your father's hospitality. Such things matter in this country as in my own. I have read *Macbeth*. I know.'

'*Macbeth*?' said Dorothy.

Joseph gave up. He sat down on the bed and spread his hands. 'Dorothy, it can't be done. I'm sorry.'

'You're mad! You really are crazy.' She went back to the door and leaned against it. 'And I'll tell you something else. You're a liar too.'

He looked up warily. 'Why do you say that?'

'All that stuff you go on about. You aren't a whatsit prince any more than I am, are you? *And* you didn't go to an English public school, either, did you?'

'Dorothy, I . . .'

'You don't have to pretend. *I'm* not stupid.'

He sighed deeply. 'Dorothy, you are a witch,' he said, in a low voice.

She opened the door and turned to go. 'Oh, don't worry. I won't grass on you. You can be King of Timbuctoo for all I care! But what I said just now, right? I won't say it again. You had your chance and you missed it. So there.'

There was something altogether peculiar in the air at Disserth House today, Daniel thought: Hunter absorbed in his plans, Dorothy walking around and slamming doors, Joseph unusually dour, Amos torturing Rose with particular sadism and Celia . . . well, Celia was just being her usual self. No one had any time for him and he wished Anita were there. He had tried to tell his parents about her that afternoon in his letter home, but it was hard to get the words right. 'Actually, O beloved ones, I have made a friend here, though it might not meet with your honourable approval! She's the cleaner here! Yes, really, though I promise that any resemblance to Mrs Fogg is purely coincidental. In fact she's taking me with her on Sunday to guess where! Her church service! She's very enthusiastic about it, only they don't call it a church. As you know, yours truly is hardly an avid churchgoer but I thought it might be good for a laugh . . .' He had not been consciously trying to lie to his parents, of course, but as he wrote, he was aware of the gap between his thoughts and the words he used to express them. He had never considered this before, and even now the gap was so infinitesimally small that it hardly seemed worth worrying about. Still, it was there.

Evening came, and to Daniel's annoyance, he seemed to be the only one around when people started arriving for Hunter's poetry reading. There was Mrs Woosnam, Mrs Potter and Mrs Rhys from the village, and he had just got them settled in the uncomfortable armchairs, when he heard a loud and penetrating voice in the hall. 'Coo-ee! Hope we're not too early! Norman's just parking the Rolls.'

'Oh,' said Daniel. 'I don't actually know where Hunter is.'

'Not to worry. We haven't met, have we? I'm Deirdre Loftus. And you must be . . . you must be . . .'

'Daniel Green.'

'Lovely to meet you, Daniel. Now where is young Celia? I've brought some extremely gooey brownies to add to the celebrations.'

Hunter now came out from his study, and Celia also appeared, framed in the kitchen door. 'Norman's just parking the Rolls,' Deirdre said. 'And I do hope you don't mind, we brought along another bod; young Jamie seemed at a loose end this evening and I know he's dying to know what dreadful things we get up to. Celia, dear, how are . . .'

'Excuse me a minute,' Celia said, 'I must just see to the . . .' She vanished again into the kitchen.

'I'll give you a hand,' called Deirdre, 'and I brought along some brownies. *Nice* to have met you,' she said encouragingly to Daniel.

'*Lo, we come with clouds* . . .' said the vicar who entered now, with a tall, gingery-haired young man. 'Ah, Hunter . . .'

Daniel found the poetry reading hugely embarrassing. After all, he had, or nearly had, an English degree, and here he was, having to listen to the vicar keeping his head when all about him, and the vicar's wife wanting to go down to the sea again. Mrs Woosnam had brought along something by Patience Strong, and horrors, claimed that she couldn't read very well, so that Daniel was roped in to read it! He, Daniel, reading Patience Strong! Sniffily, he read an especially obscure bit of 'Ash Wednesday' when his own turn came round and hoped everyone hated it.

Celia was, or should have been next. Though funnily enough, she seemed to be quite flustered this evening. 'Oh, I can't . . . I er . . .'

'Really, Celia, we must all pull our weight,' Hunter said sternly.

Then Jamie Loftus, the vicar's son, who had said very little so far, spoke. 'I've got a poem,' he said. 'Perhaps I could . . .'

'Splendid!' said Hunter. 'At least someone's bothered. I hope you feel thoroughly put to shame, Celia.'

'Perhaps I'll just get some more coffee,' Celia muttered.

'Stay where you are. You'd be very rude if you walked out on poor Jamie.'

'No, please, really,' said Jamie. 'It's just one I found in an old school book. I'm not really much of a poetry man myself.'

'There's no such animal,' said Hunter, 'as these little evenings try to prove. We can all enjoy poetry. All right, Jamie, let's hear you.'

Jamie glanced round the room. 'It's by John Donne, actually,' he said.

'Ah yes,' said Norman. '*Send not to know* . . . Marvellous stuff.'

'I think he wrote this before he became a vicar,' Jamie said. His voice sounded hesitant. 'It's about love,' he added, more firmly.

Deirdre regarded her son with pride. An expectant, polite, silence fell.

Now the only sound to be heard was Jamie's young, light voice, stiff at first, but growing in confidence as he spoke:

> *'So, so, break off this last lamenting kiss,*
> *Which sucks two souls and vapours both away . . .'*

Daniel noticed that Celia appeared to be having some trouble with her coffee cup, which must surely be empty by now. It clattered noisily against the saucer.

> *'Turn thou ghost that way, and let me turn this,*
> *And let ourselves benight our happiest day.'*

Now Celia had something in her throat. She started to cough.

> *'We asked none leave to love, nor will we owe*
> *Any, so cheap a death as saying, Go . . .'*

Celia's coughing fit, quiet at first, became so loud as to drown out Jamie's voice. She rose clumsily to her feet, 'I'm so sorry.'

'So you should be,' Hunter reproved. 'You've just spoiled a very creditable piece of reading.'

'I'm so sorry, I . . .'

'It's quite all right, Mrs Hunter, please don't worry,' said Jamie.

'I've told you before Celia won't mind you calling her by her Christian name, Jamie, you silly ha'p'orth,' said Deirdre. 'Are you all right, Celia dear?'

'Yes, I'm fine,' mumbled Celia, scarlet-faced. 'I'll just . . .' And she fled from the room.

'I'm so sorry,' said Hunter. 'Do carry on, Jamie.'

But he read the last verse in a flat monotonous voice. Daniel recognized the tone in which he had conducted the odd conversation about the Jacob's wool. Moreover, the way Jamie read, getting all the pauses in the wrong place, made nonsense of all that stuff about murderers. It was quite clear that he didn't know a thing about poetry. So what was he doing, reading a love poem? And the way Jamie looked at Celia when she fled the room!

The suspicion, already planted, began to grow. Something fishy was definitely going on here.

Surely not *that*? But if not, then what?

Oh, if only he had Anita to talk to!

Chapter 8

'There's nothing *wrong* in it,' Daniel told himself. 'It's not as though I want to do anything *wrong*.'

He had rehearsed this several times to himself that Sunday morning after breakfast, but the more he told himself that he was doing nothing wrong — and logically, surely he wasn't — the more he felt that he was.

Perhaps it was just the prospect of telling Hunter. For he was aware, though without quite knowing why, that Hunter would disapprove of his going.

And, no, of course, Hunter did not approve.

'*Anita*?'

'You know Anita, she comes here on . . .'

'I know who Anita is, Daniel. I want to know why you've made this arrangement without consulting me.'

'I'm sorry, Hunter, but I wanted to go, and I am.'

So there.

Anita came, not on the dreaded motorbike, but in a little white Mini. 'Mike lent it to me.' Like all confident people, she peppered her conversation with names she did not bother to explain.

When he told her about his conversation with Hunter, she was inclined to laugh it off. 'Oh, you must expect that sort of thing, I'm afraid.' She looked so nice this morning, in pale lilac, skirt and blouse freshly ironed; unlike Dorothy who had shambled blearily down to breakfast in a grubby outsize T-shirt, traces of last night's mascara under her eyes. It was not unpleasant to be driving away from Disserth House, fast (rather too fast, but Anita's confidence in God was reassuring) through the snarled and bowery greenness of the lanes. God deposited them in Llanafon unscathed and they drove through the town centre into a quiet road lined with large Victorian villas, which were now flats, hotels and conference centres. Anita drove into a sweeping drive and stopped the car so that the tyres squeaked on the gravel. 'Here we are,' she said as proudly as if she were displaying her ancestral mansion. 'What do you think of it?'

What did he think of it? 'Very nice, Anita.' For what else could you say? The big house, gabled and turreted, had been modernized cleanly and neatly, with a good deal of wood and plate glass. Over the new door, a sign read, 'The Fellowship of Saints.'

'Not like some of those — excuse me, Daniel — gloomy old places. I went into the church at St Rhuna and quite frankly, you could smell the damp, and I think there were bats there. Just wait till you see our Meeting House.'

The Meeting House was a modern hall next to the old house. Inside were rows of stacking chairs and white painted walls. The wooden floor shone as glossy as barley sugar and a big jug of yellow daisies stood on the altar — though was it an altar if this was not a church? He did not like to ask.

The Meeting House was already full of people and Anita introduced him. He had an impression of clean, smiling faces and bright eyes. Many of the men wore beards, but not scruffy ones; the women were dressed in the soft, fresh colours that Anita wore; fondant pink and lemon sorbet, delphinium blue and almond green. He could not remember all the names, but there was a Mike and a Phil and a Dave; there were Sue and Lynn and Pam and Anne. Saint

Dave, Saint Sue? He wanted to giggle at this but he knew Anita would not find it amusing. Many of them lived in the Fellowship House, but he could hear no Welsh accents. Nothing about the saints seemed to link them to any group of people he had known or heard about before; it was almost as though they had all been landed, smiling and shining, from another planet, a place where the flowers always blossomed and the sun always shone.

'It isn't always easy, brothers and sisters,' said Mike, who appeared to be the — what? The vicar? priest? minister? Or something quite different — the Fellowship needed brand-new words to define it. 'It's not always easy to stand up in this modern world as His witnesses must do . . .' Then he told a story about a Saint who had been taking a long, late night train journey to Scotland, when a man opposite, bleary-eyed, had offered him a swig from a gin bottle. Mike told the story rather well, and Daniel was so entranced that he could almost smell the eggy stale air of the carriage and feel his eyelids prickling with late night exhaustion. The Saint refused the drink, left a pamphlet behind, and got off at Glasgow. His fellow passenger, who had been planning an adulterous weekend, read the pamphlet, gave up the booze and went back to his wife instead. Now both worked for the Fellowship. Daniel listened to the end and only then remembered that a moral tale had been unfolding. He wished Mike would tell them another one, but they sang a jolly hymn about Love.

After the Meeting, Anita took him into the Fellowship House for lunch. Inside, the house was all white walls, clean Scandinavian furniture and cheerful curtains. 'It's all very comfy, isn't it?' she said proudly, and he had to agree. In fact, it was just the sort of place Disserth House should have been, not full of saggy chairs and bits of Lego. If he had come to a place like this to recover from his whatever-it-was, then he might have been feeling better already. Mike, with his smile and vigorous handshake, might almost have been a younger, more streamlined version of Hunter himself, and you could be pretty sure Jean, his wife, would never let her children call anyone a 'fuckie'.

Lunch was served, by the women, in the dining-room, where about twenty-five people sat down at long tables covered with gingham cloths. Delicious lunch it was, too, although everything had been prepared the night before. ('For of course we don't cook on the Sabbath, Daniel.') Everyone talked to him and he tried to remember the names; but it did not seem to matter much; no one was testing him or sizing him up, he felt, they just wanted to communicate their excitement. And indeed, he had never known a meal where such intense talking went on, while morsels of food perched on waving forks. At first, he just wanted to get on with eating, but then he found that his food, too, was uneaten.

'You see, Daniel, it's so exciting and it's going to happen *any moment now*!'

'All the signs are there, the earthquakes, the famines.'

'This generation shall not pass away. We're so privileged!'

The event which filled them with so much excitement was, in fact, the end of the world, something which Daniel had never thought of before as a cause for great enthusiasm, yet they spoke of it with glowing eyes and shining faces. Perhaps it really was going to be like a big party. Moreover, and this was the bit that impressed Daniel, everything they said could be backed up with quotations from the Bible. Quotations meant evidence and evidence meant that it must be so. This much, Daniel knew for sure.

All around him, the air crackled and fizzed and sparkled, so that he could not help but be charged by it. By the time the end of the meal came with ice-cream and chocolate cake, he could not imagine how anyone could possibly disagree with such a way of looking at things.

'Such a pretty town!' Anita said. 'And I've been so happy here!'

Now it was three o'clock in the afternoon and Daniel and Anita had gone for a walk in Llanafon. They had found a tea-room and were sitting inside, among the corn dollies and horse brasses, being served by a middle-aged woman in a flowery smock.

Daniel tried to think of Llanafon as a pretty town. He had not seen it as such before, but now Anita mentioned it, he could see she was right.

And then . . . oh, then! . . . she leaned across the table to him, and said, 'It's been really lovely having you here, Daniel. I can't remember when I've enjoyed my dinner so much.'

Well! What could he say to that? 'It's been really great, Anita.'

'You know, the first time we met, I had a feeling in my bones that we were going to be friends — *special* friends, I mean.'

Daniel had always considered that the world held two categories of people; the first, very large, to whom nice things happened, and the second, much smaller (consisting, in fact, now he came to think of it, only of himself), to whom they did not. Yet this was all so easy. It was like finding yourself suddenly able to skate like a champion; all the exhilaration without the work, for he was suddenly having . . . well, it had to be said, a very particular kind of conversation with Anita. He wondered if the two middle-aged ladies opposite were aware of it.

Anita told him about how she had come to the Fellowship and how marvellous it was and how her great ambition was to go to India, for, 'Can you imagine anything more dreadful, Daniel, a great country like that where nearly everybody is going to be damned?' Of course, she added, she wouldn't be able to go straight away, for missionaries in the Fellowship were usually married couples. It put all those . . . you know . . . temptations behind you, and after all, God intended people to marry, and though perhaps it was a bit improper to speak of it now, married love was, by all accounts, such a wonderful thing! Then she said, 'Oh, Daniel, if only you, too, would find the Lord, what a wonderful thing it would be. You know, now that we've become such friends, I can hardly bear to imagine you not being among the Chosen Ones!'

Daniel thought about this. Yes, indeed, it would be pretty dreadful. It would mean, in fact, being in Hell, though Anita did not mention this in so many words. If he had a friend, he would surely not like to think of that friend going to . . . there was no other word for it . . . Hell.

Now their tea arrived, and with it a plate of home-made cakes. 'Yummy!' said Anita with enthusiasm, for being a Saint did not seem to exclude cream cakes. He thought of what she had said about the pleasures of married love and a thrill ran through him.

So enthralled was he, that it was not until they were on their way back to the Fellowship House that he re-membered Celia.

'Anita, you know the other day, you said there was something funny going on with Mrs Hunter and the knitting? Well, I think you might be right.' And he told her about the poetry reading. Anita was interested straight away.

'*How* did James Loftus look at Mrs Hunter, Daniel?'

'Well, you know. In that way.'

'As though they were lovers, you mean?'

Yes, he supposed he did.

'And you're suggesting he read that poem as a private message to Mrs Hunter?'

Yes, he supposed he meant that too.

'Do you know what this implies, Daniel?'

He looked at her, goggle-eyed. No, he had not quite thought that one out yet.

But Anita had. 'You're suggesting that Mrs Hunter is

having . . . or is thinking of having . . . an adulterous relationship with James Loftus . . .'

'Adulterous?'

'Well, how else would you describe it, Daniel?'

'I don't know. Yes, like that, I suppose.'

'And I must say, I've noticed that Mrs Hunter's been even vaguer than usual lately. She's *always* asking me to look after the children while she . . . Daniel, I think we've uncovered something very serious here.'

'Yes, I think so too,' he said, glad that he had made such an impression.

'The trouble is, we haven't enough to go on. We'll need proof.'

'*Proof*?' The word fell awkwardly and oddly into the conversation.

'Well, we can't go accusing someone without proof, can we?'

'But do we have to . . . I mean, I didn't think . . .'

She turned towards him a face that was a grave Victorian mask of Honour and Justice. 'Daniel, you surely don't imagine that we can just turn aside from this, if this is true, do you?'

'Well, it really isn't our business, is it? I mean I know it's bad and all that but . . .'

'We're talking about *adultery*, Daniel.'

'Well, yes, I suppose so, but . . .'

'There's no point pretending we don't know of such things, though, my goodness, I wish we didn't have to, but there it is. We're talking about adultery and that, Daniel, is a very grave crime against God. For a woman it's about as bad as it can be. You know that, don't you?'

'Yes, but . . .'

'I'm surprised you think there are any buts about it.'

'Well, I don't, of course I don't, but . . .'

'So what are you trying to tell me?'

'No. Nothing. Nothing at all.'

'God will show us the way,' she said calmly. 'We can watch and we can pray and God will tell us what to do. Of course, I hope, really hope, that everything turns out to be a misunderstanding. No one will be happier than me, believe me, but if it doesn't, and Mrs Hunter really is doing this dreadful thing, then there's only one course of action.'

'What?' he asked humbly.

'What?' Cool blue eyes, sapphires, mountain pools, forget-me-nots unwavering. 'What? Why, Daniel, we have no choice. We must tell Mr Hunter!'

Chapter 9

Celia's day started badly. First of all, Joseph tried to persuade her to cash a cheque for him. 'You see, Mrs Hunter, in just a few days, my allowance will have come through and by the time you pay the cheque in, it will be cleared and all will be well.'

'But Joseph, I haven't *got* twenty pounds.'

'Fifteen?'

'I'm sorry.'

'Ten? Seven?'

In the end, just to shut him up, she gave him five, though she knew she would probably never see it again and Charlie needed new shoes. Joseph went off praising her goodness. He was followed by Hunter, not pleased. 'Celia, for God's sake, can't you do something about these?' He held out a stack of brightly coloured pamphlets: *Satan And You*, *His Word Is The Law*, *God Is Not Mocked*. 'I found them all over the living-room.'

'Oh. It looks like Anita.'

'Of course it's Anita, but the point is, it wasn't Anita who left these there, it was Daniel. God only knows what she put into his head yesterday.'

'Oh, dear.'

'Celia, is that all you can say?'

'What do you expect me to say?'

'Sometimes,' he said carefully, 'I think you behave like

this on purpose to annoy me. What I expect you to say, dearest Celia, is to tell Anita that this sort of thing can't be tolerated.'

'Couldn't you tell her?'

'Why can't you?'

'Because she doesn't like me,' Celia said helplessly. 'She doesn't do anything I say.'

'Doesn't *like* you? Doesn't *do anything you say*? Celia, are you the mistress of this house or not?'

'Yes, but . . .'

'Then the best thing you can do is tell Anita we no longer have need for her services. That young lady is fast becoming a major pain in the neck.'

'You mean give her notice?'

'Exactly.'

'But . . .'

'But, Celia?'

'Hunter, I can't. I mean, we need her help for your St Rhuna's Day thing. She promised to come and help with the food.'

Hunter thought about it. 'Very well. She can stay as long as that. Then she's out. And you, dearest chuck, are going to be the one to tell her so.'

But Celia did not spend much time thinking about Anita, except to wonder, how, with Anita not there, she could manage to get away as often. Today was her day for taking the market garden produce into Llanafon, and this time she had left the children with Sally Price of Coed Farm. ('There really isn't room for them in the car with all the lettuces.') Without Anita, there would be one excuse less. Yet her arrangements for meeting Jamie, so careful at first, but which lately had become more reckless, had apparently aroused no suspicions in Hunter; perhaps he was too distracted with his festival. It seemed that whatever she wanted to do, she could get away with.

When she arrived at the cave, Jamie was already there. At

first, she could sense rather than see him, a dark shape in the darkness, his breathing swift and anxious, the warmth of his body masking the malodorous air of the cave. There, they had set up their own magic kingdom so when she fell into his arms, all her everyday problems became trivial and irrelevant, and if she thought of Hunter at all, it was as of someone she had known in another world. As they made love she was a queen, a goddess, her life no longer a confusion. The feeling might be short-lived and it might be illusory, but while it lasted it made everything else worth-while.

'Listen, I've got good news,' he said afterwards.

'What?' she murmured into his ear. His skin tasted hot and salty.

'Well, the first thing is, I've got this interview with ICI.'

'In London?'

'Yes.'

'I thought you said good news,' she said, drawing away from him.

'It is when you hear the next bit. Listen carefully. There are these friends of friends who have a house in Muswell Hill, right? They're going to Saudi Arabia on a two-year contract and they want to let the house cheaply to someone who'll house-sit for them.'

'Yes, but . . .'

'See? Didn't I say I'd find a way? I'm Magic Man, Celia. I can do anything.'

'You're saying we should go and live in this house?'

'While we look for something permanent.'

'What about Charlie and . . .'

'. . . Amos and Rose? I know. They come, too, of course. What else did you think I meant?'

'But . . .'

'There you go again. But what?'

'I don't know. It just seems to be too easy.'

'He's really brainwashed you, hasn't he?' said Jamie. 'Got

you quite conditioned to the idea that *you're* not allowed to be happy. Well, it's not going to be that way any more. You *are* going to be happy. We both are. He's not going to get away with it any more. I promise you. Oh, Celia, my love, soon we're going to be together for the rest of our lives.'

'This letter,' said Professor Green. 'It just does not sound like a letter from my son.'

Professor Green's common room colleagues were becoming just a little fed up with Professor Green's son. Dr J P Hardiment (Carolingian and Romanesque) stirred Coffee-Mate into his paper cup and yawned. 'They're young, Frieda. They just want to do their own thing. You have to leave them to get on with it.' Dr Hardiment's son was at present getting on with marijuana, squatting in Lambeth and the Animal Liberation Front. Privately, the Hardiments called Daniel The Boy Wonder and felt his present behaviour made things fairer all round.

'Pardon me, Jack,' said the Professor. 'Leaving them to get on with it has never been my philosophy. You see, I love my son.'

'Oh, for heaven's sake, we all *love* our sons.' He made the word sound like some embarrassing mental aberration.

'Then why,' persisted Professor Green, 'if we love them so, do they go off the railings?'

Dr Hardiment giggled. He did enjoy it when the Professor's grasp of English idiom occasionally slipped.

'It's just a phase. A temporary phase.' So far, Luke Hardiment's temporary phase had endured six years. 'I say, do you know who it is who keeps nicking the *New York Review of Books*? I never get a chance to clap eyes on it these days.'

'I think you'll find it's Peter,' said Colin MacNaughton (Cleary Fellow of Ethnic Minority Studies). 'He seems to be undergoing one of his periodic nervous breakdowns.

99

Stealing newspapers is apparently essential to his peace of mind.'

'Well, it's not doing my peace of mind any good,' grumbled Dr Hardiment. 'I haven't even seen Clausewitz's review yet. Bugger Peter.'

'Oh, what a good idea,' squealed Colin, who might have been gay, or who perhaps might only have made a pretence of it.

'I am trying to talk about something serious,' said the Professor, 'and all you can offer is frivolity. I am talking of my son, about whom I am seriously worried. This letter is like that of a zombie. Look: *I have spent a most interesting morning studying my Bible, and I really feel I've made some important discoveries.* This is not the language of my son.'

'The trouble with you, dear Frieda,' said Colin, 'is that you're too good. You expect everyone else to be good, and honestly, they're not. They're rotten bastards, most of them.'

'What has goodness to do with it? I do not expect goodness from anyone.'

'What Colin means,' said Jack, 'is just leave him alone and young Daniel will find his own level, I promise.'

'You are in no position to make promises about Daniel's level,' the Professor said huffily. 'I am worried and I consider I have a right to be worried, but as obviously no one wishes to listen to me, in future, I shall keep my worries to myself.'

'I say,' said Jack Hardiment, 'isn't that old Wallenby coming in? Good Lord. I thought he'd snuffed it.'

Colin giggled. 'From the look of him, I'd say he had; years ago, I'd say.'

Dorothy made her way to the top field with *Princess Daisy* tucked under her arm. The heat had increased her lethargy; if only she could have stayed in bed all day, but, of course, Hunter would never stand for *that*. In the house, Joseph attempted to impress her with some discovery he had made about Celtic symbolism, Daniel asked her opinion on Original Sin, Celia, with a dazed face, was slowly and languorously doing the ironing. There was no solace to be had from anyone there.

Outside, she found nothing to improve her temper, though the air was heavy with the scent of meadowsweet and the sky was deeply blue. Pavements and shops were what she wanted to see.

The top meadow was empty and she flung herself down on the grass, which felt damp, although it had not rained for a long time. Little flies buzzed in an insistent cloud around her head, there was the sour smell of sheep dung. The more distant beauties of the view, the intense, soaked emerald of the grass, the transparent ultramarine shimmer of the far-off hills did not touch her. 'I hate this bloody place,' she said out loud.

Princess Daisy was proving hard to get into. At home, hidden under the bed in case Hunter saw them, were a pile of Mills & Boons, with swooning girls on the cover. Hunter, of course, did not approve of such things. Once he'd thrown nearly ten quid's worth of paperbacks borrowed from Julie Rees into the Aga. Dorothy closed *Princess Daisy* and began to dream about the man into whose arms she would swoon. He had a suntan all over and he was blonde, with short hair and blue eyes. He was wearing white shorts and his feet were bare. He would never have to put on socks or a tie for he lived in a wonderful climate where the sun always shone; a hedonistic beach land. His bottom was very small and firm and she put herself to the task of wondering what it would be like when he wriggled, ever so gracefully, out of those white shorts.

At that point, there was a noise in the distance. A dog barked fussily and the sheep, which had been peacefully grazing, scattered and began to bunch awkwardly. Even a movement of sheep broke the tedium. She raised herself up on her elbows to watch.

Into the field by the top gate came Kevin, riding a white horse. The Joneses kept several horses in conditions that scandalized Deirdre and used them quite often for odd jobs round the farm. Kevin had sat all his life on horses without self-consciousness or effort. He rode this afternoon bareback and bareheaded, his white shirt carelessly unbuttoned.

He waved an arm in her direction, but otherwise took no notice of her. Kevin at work was quite a different animal from Kevin at rest. The sheep had to be moved into another field, and she watched as he went about the work, snapping commands in a sharp staccato. Hunter had once told her that these words of command used by hill-farmers went back thousands of years, to a language that was older than English or Welsh. A Stone-Age Kevin might have moved and called just as he did. The dog ran and crouched and slithered, fussing at the sheep with little delicate movements, while they protested with loud bleating.

Now the sun, which had momentarily vanished behind a cloud, came out again, and in the same instant Kevin rode full into its beam. The sky shone with luminous intensity and Kevin, astride his horse, blazed into sudden beauty, his hair becoming a deep bronzed gold, his reddish Celtic skin glowing richest terracotta. All along his arms, the fair hairs shone as if he had been powdered with gold dust. Throwing his head back, his arms tensed on the reins, his muscles working, he might have been a young knight approaching the Grail, or a prince riding into battle. Dorothy pulled herself up to stare at this unexpected apotheosis. 'Hey, Kev!' she called.

But a young god has no time for mortal women. 'Shut up, Dorothy, I'm busy, aren't I?'

'Ke-ev!' she pleaded.

'Shut up, girl.'

'In a minute, then!'

'Oh, all right. Hey, Sally, *Sally!*' This was to the sheepdog who had sensed his brief inattention and pretended to be losing control. Dorothy sighed and sank back on to the grass. Sally snapped back into action; the sheep bunched and collided with each other; then suddenly the leader got the message and ran bleating indignantly through the gate. First one, then another, followed and then, while Kevin jumped from his horse and shut the gate, the rest blundered through in an awkward mass. Then, slightly to her surprise, he came striding across the field in her direction. But the sun had gone behind a cloud and with it the wonderful coppery-gold hero.

'What you want then, girl?'

She sighed, crossly. But that brief transcendental moment of glory had done its stuff. 'Sit down. Let's talk.'

'Think I've got nothing better to do than gossip with you all day? There's loads of bales waiting for me to cart them.' But he sat down.

'I'm pissed off,' said Dorothy. She rammed *Princess Daisy* so hard down on its front that the spine cracked audibly. 'I'm bored. I hate this bloody place.'

'Wouldn't mind having the time to be bored sometimes,' he said.

'Oh, Kevin, don't be so sanctimonious. Let's have it off.'

Kevin jumped as though a few thousand volts had gone through him. '*What?*'

'You heard.'

'I'm not sure I did.'

'God, do I have to spell it out?'

'No, but Dorothy . . . bloody hell.'

'I don't think much of that for an answer.'

'Bloody hell!'

'You said that already.'

'You mean . . . you and me . . . here? You mean . . .'

'I mean you and me here,' said Dorothy firmly. 'Or did you want to include the bloody dog?'

'Blimey, girl, don't talk so dirty. You want me to . . .'

103

'I want you to do it. To me. Here,' Dorothy said wearily, 'All a bit sudden, this.'

'Sudden? Oh, you hypocrite, Kevin, don't tell me you haven't thought about it.'

'*Thought* about it, course I *thought* about it. Blimey! But Dorothy . . .'

'Then you're scared,' Dorothy said. 'That's what you are.'

'No, I'm not.'

'Or perhaps you're gay, that's why.'

'*Gay*? You mean I'm a bloody poof? Is that what you mean? Blimey, I'll show you bloody poof.'

'Well, *show* me then. That's what I'm asking you to do.'

'Look here, I can't just . . .'

'You just said you could.'

'Well, I *could*, course I *could*. But . . . damn, it's not that simple.'

'Course it's simple. You just take your trousers off and I . . .'

'Shut up, girl, you don't have to tell me that. I know what to *do*, but . . .'

Dorothy sat up and pulled her skirt down to her knees. 'You can't, or you won't, or you don't want to. Well, thank you very much, Kevin.'

'Look, don't be like that, Dorothy.' His eyes took on a sly expression. 'Tell you what, we'll go out tonight. I'll meet you by the back gate; don't tell your dad, and we'll take the Land Rover.'

'Oh, no,' she said. 'If you think you're getting me in the back of a smelly Land Rover, you've another think coming. No, you've had your chance.'

'Dorothy . . .'

'This offer now closes. You turned it down when it was offered to you, and so that's it. Sorry. It's back to sheep-buggering for you, Kev.'

★

Joseph, poor and anxious, was in a bad mood. In the living-room, Daniel Green looked up at him from the armchair with an unusually sunny smile.

'I say, Joseph,' he said. 'Have you ever read the Bible?'

'Of course I have read the Bible,' said Joseph, in what was for him, a nasty tone of voice. 'Missionaries would trade them for glass beads and bits of mirror.'

But today's smiling Daniel was immune to sarcasm. 'It's really very interesting. Don't you agree? I never realized there was so much in it.'

Outside, the sun shone blindingly and a flock of midges hovered in a little cloud. From behind a clump of trees came the creak of a swinging sunbed. The creaking was querulous, insistent. It sounded like — it probably was — Dorothy. Since to all Joseph's problems was now added a sudden surge of sexual desire, it seemed inappropriate to encounter Dorothy.

He had — all that was left to him in the world — about three pounds fifty. He went down the path, through the gate and down the road on his way to the shop. On his way, he met Mrs Woosnam. 'Oh, good afternoon, Mr Um-ah-um,' she said. 'Hot enough for you? Still I don't expect you mind this weather, do you?'

Time to move on, thought Joseph, time to go.

Chapter 10

'Work first, then fun, Daniel,' said Anita. 'I finish at twelve today, then we can have a walk and a little chat.' Today, Anita's pink skirt was scattered with a design of white rabbits. Dorothy's dress looked as though it had been mangled in the washing machine and then used to line a cat basket.

Faint as a wraith, Celia came out of the kitchen, a piece of toast in her hand. 'Oh, by the way, Anita, I wanted a word . . .' she began, and then quavered to a halt. 'Of course, you're busy now, I can see.'

Anita returned a glacial smile. 'I'm never too busy to listen, Mrs Hunter. Was it . . . something special . . . you wanted to say to me?'

'Oh, no, it can wait.'

'There's always prayer, Mrs Hunter,' said Anita. 'You'll find it works wonders. You try it; don't just take my word for it.'

'Thank you,' said Celia in astonishment. She blinked, then vanished palely into the kitchen. The air closed over her presence. Anita watched, eyes narrowed.

'Gosh,' said Daniel, who had not yet quite worked out how he should be taking all this.

'*Such is the way,*' quoted Anita softly, '*of an adulterous woman. She eateth and wipeth her mouth, and saith, I have done no wickedness. Proverbs, thirty, verse twenty.*'

'Gosh,' said Daniel again.

But then Anita smiled at him and his world flowered into sunshine. 'Still, we mustn't let her affect our happiness, must we? Why don't I meet you here at twelve and we'll go for a nice walk down by that pretty little stream, shall we?'

In the living-room Joseph picked up a pile of bright pamphlets and leafed through them with interest. 'This,' he said to the creeper that clung in green tendrils at the window, 'is what I need. I need a Redeemer. I need to be redeemed from my sins and make a fresh start. But how can such a thing be possible?'

'Not at all,' said Hunter over the phone. 'Two o'clock, in three days' time, the fourteenth. Just a little ceremony to . . . Oh, no, I've invented nothing . . . certainly, the more the merrier. In the afternoon? Oh, some games, a dance. Ysbadadden are coming. No that's Ysbadadden, a folk group. Y-s-b . . . yes, that's it. I'm hoping someone from the BBC . . . what? Oh, to regenerate as it were the holiness with which St Rhuna imbued the place by her life and her . . . yes, that's it. Rhuna. R-h-u . . .'

'Ssh,' said Celia, some time later into the same phone. 'Ten thirty. Yes, they'll all be too busy. Of course. Ssh. Not for long, though. Yes, I do too. Oh, *darling*.'

She did not hear, as she put the phone down, the gentle click on the extension.

Kevin was hanging around the boundary fields making a nuisance of himself. 'What you said, Dorothy,' he pleaded, 'what you said the other day.'

'That was the other day,' Dorothy said firmly.

'Look here,' he said belligerently, 'you can't go round like that. All Come-On-Darling one minute and Little-Miss-Touch-Me-Not the next.'

'I can do exactly what I like.'

'There's a name for girls like you, that's all,' Kevin continued, trying to blunder his way into her heart.

'There's a name for blokes like you too.'

'Well, that's all very well, isn't it?' said Kevin. In fact, he had to shout it as Dorothy turned to go. 'Girls like you ought to have their bottoms smacked, they ought. Well, you can't muck about with me, I'm telling you. You're going to find out, all you bloody poncy stuck-up English are going to find out . . .'

But Dorothy never heard what it was she was going to find out as she had already disappeared into the willows by the side of the stream that separated Hunter's land from Jones territory.

She did, however, bump into Daniel and Anita. Daniel, ducking beneath an overhanging branch, had little pieces of leaf stuck in his hair. 'Oh,' said Dorothy. 'What are you two up to, then?'

Daniel giggled. 'Up to?' said Anita pleasantly. 'Now what did you mean by that, Dorothy?'

'Up to,' said Dorothy. 'Naughtiness. Nooky. Hanky-panky. Nudge nudge wink wink.'

Daniel, to his eternal discredit, giggled again. Anita did not. 'I'm afraid I can't imagine what you mean. Daniel and I are going for a little walk. Only a twisted mind could see anything wrong in that.'

'Leave him alone, can't you?' said Dorothy. 'You're the one with the twisted mind. He doesn't know what you're up to.'

'Hey, look here,' Daniel growled. But Anita, like a glittering lady knight in stainless steel armour leapt to his defence. *If any man defile the temple of God, him shall God destroy. I should think about that, Dorothy. I should think about it quite hard if I were you.'*

Dorothy turned to Daniel. For a moment, she looked at him quite kindly. 'Daniel, can't you see she's mad? Leave her alone. Come back to the house with me.'

'Don't you listen to her,' Anita said.

'Anyway, it's lunchtime, and you know what Hunter's like about people being late for lunch.'

'Perhaps I shouldn't miss lunch.' Daniel turned helplessly to Anita.

'I thought about lunch,' Anita said coldly. 'I've made us a nice little picnic, Daniel. There's no need for you to go back to the house.'

'But Hunter might . . .'

'Mr Hunter won't mind you talking to me.'

'For God's sake,' Dorothy said, 'can't you *see* what she's trying to do to you?'

Daniel looked at the two girls, Anita in white and pink, her eyes forget-me-not blue, Dorothy with her rumpled hair and cat's basket dress. But there was a warmth coming from her and a scent of flowers and her mouth was open and moist.

'Daniel!'

'Don't listen to her, Daniel.'

For a moment he hesitated between the two. He knew really which one he would obey, but for a moment glimpsed a ravishing skein of possibilities if he made the other choice.

'Er . . . you go back to the house, Dorothy. I'll stay with Anita, if you don't mind.'

He hoped she would continue to persuade him otherwise, but all she said was, 'Sod you then, you can go to hell if you like, see if I care,' and was off. He watched the bright flashes of colour as she moved between bushes, then she was gone.

'Well!' said Anita. 'What a terrible thing to say. What sort of a mind could think up a thing like that, Daniel? Still, let's just forget it all, shall we, and have our little picnic? I've got some nice baps and some pop. And Sue made us melting moments.'

Daniel did not know what any of these things were, but it would all be delicious. In this strange new land he was entering with Anita, even the words were different.

'Quite honestly,' Anita was saying, 'if you don't mind me saying, I really think you're better off away from that house. Of course, if it were all up to Mr Hunter, things would be different. But with that . . . that *woman* in charge of things,

and young Dorothy flaunting herself . . . And that coloured gentleman doesn't seem to be quite all there if you'll
pardon the expression.'

'Oh, they're a funny lot,' he agreed.

'A *bad* lot,' she corrected gently. 'Well, never mind, it
won't be for much longer.'

'No.'

'Just until we can make the arrangements . . .'

'Arrangements?'

'Why, for you to come and live in the Fellowship
House.'

'The Fellowship House?' he repeated, a little faintly.

She turned to him in surprise. 'You *do* want to become
one of us, don't you, Daniel?'

'Oh, yes I do, but . . .'

'Phew. For a minute I thought that we might have our
lines crossed there. What a relief, thank goodness.'

'It's just that I hadn't quite realized . . .'

'Now, there's egg and cress or salmon and cucumber.
Personally, I'd go for the salmon. What hadn't you quite
realized?'

'Oh, nothing really.'

'Well, I'm glad everything's all right. You see,' she said,
lowering her eyes. 'I have my own special little reason for
looking forward to the day you join us. I expect you can
guess what it is, can't you?'

Could he? He looked at her, then at the stream, then
back at her again. Could he? She reached out a hand and
just ever so gently, brushed his with it. 'We *are* just a bit
. . . you know, special, aren't we?'

In that moment, he quite forgot Dorothy. 'Oh, yes,
Anita. Oh, yes.'

'And for people like you and me, there can only be one
answer, can't there?'

Utterly lost, but quite happy, he replied, 'Oh, yes.
Absolutely.'

She shifted her position and leaned back, tilting her pretty white neck and chin. 'Oh, I'm so glad, Daniel, so happy. One day, quite soon, you'll be coming to live at the Fellowship and then . . . Oh, doesn't it make you excited, just to think of it?'

'Oh, yes, definitely. But Anita, what . . .'

'Of course, there's no reason for a long engagement, is there, once you're as certain as we are. Long engagements only . . . well, you know. We wouldn't want things to be like that, would we?'

Suddenly he realized what she was talking about. An engagement? Engaged? *Engaged*? Engaged to Anita? Was he? Is this how things happened? Surely there should have been some other bits in between. Didn't people go in for . . . well, kissing and things like that before they got engaged? Engaged to Anita!

Well. Bloody hell. No, not bloody hell, that was rude. But . . .

Gosh.

He ate a salmon roll without being aware of it. Then an egg and cress. Then another. He took a swig of warm, metallic dandelion and burdock from the bottle.

Engaged to Anita.

'Are you sure?' he said. 'You don't want to change your mind?'

'Oh, you old funny boots! You don't think I'd change my mind so quickly, do you?'

'No, oh, no, of course not, but . . .'

'I shall always remember this moment,' she said. 'This nice stream and the little birds singing and all the lovely flowers. This place will always be special to me.'

'And to me too. Certainly.'

'So lovely and quiet. Daniel?' She laughed and hid her face behind her hand. 'Now that we're nearly . . . you know . . . can I tell you a little secret? One day, not very long ago, when I'd finished work for the day, I came down to this little place by the stream and it was so hot and so lovely and so . . . quiet, do you know what I did, Daniel?'

'What?'

'Well!' She giggled prettily into her hand. 'I'm afraid I was rather a naughty girl. You see, I took all my clothes off and I stood there in the stream. It was so quiet you see. Oh dear!'

'You mean . . .' he said slowly. 'It was you . . . it was . . .'

'Oh,' she said, 'I've made you angry, haven't I?'

'No, of course not. It's just . . .'

'I have. I've offended you. I wouldn't do that for the world. But I did want you to know, because we should have no secrets from each other, should we? It was a bad thing, but there was no one to see, except God, and of course I have no secrets from *Him*; He's there even in our most intimate moments, isn't He?'

As though God was even now reading his mind, Daniel moved away from Anita.

'I have upset you, just a teeny bit, haven't I, telling you that?'

'No, Anita, really.' For he could not, of course, tell her. He could never tell her. Just one little secret, and then no more, just as she had said it would be.

'You see,' she went on, 'it was so hot and sticky and the water looked so cool! And really, Daniel, you must believe that I've kept myself pure. I know God isn't really cross about what I did. I just stood in the stream, my feet were *freezing*, Daniel, honestly, but the rest of me was lovely and warm, and I just sort of said *thank you*, God, for giving me all this lovely world. Of course, I hadn't met you then, or I would have thanked him for that, too. Oh, isn't it wonderful to think about us, Daniel! They say married love is such a wonderful thing! One flesh, Daniel, that's what the Lord said. They shall become as one flesh. When I was little, I used to wonder what that meant. I used to think of

Elastoplast, you know, flesh-coloured, it sounded funny. My parents, bless them, said, you'll understand about it some day, in God's good time.'

Daniel swallowed. He was finding it very hard to talk. 'What you said about long engagements,' he managed to say, 'you don't think they're a good . . .'

'Better to marry than to burn,' she said softly. 'Oh, we know what it's like to burn, don't we?'

Did he not? In fact, at this moment, he felt as though Mount Vesuvius had just erupted on top of him. Oh, he burned all right! And the more he thought about that slender white body in the stream, the more he burned. No secrets. No secrets. Well, one could not harm, could it? He would hoard that image in his head until the day when . . . it all seemed too good to be true. Anita . . . and all that . . . his for the asking.

He leaned over to her and tried to take her by the wrist. His mouth and tongue seemed to have swollen up and the blood pumped sluggishly in his veins.

But she pushed him away, and when he looked at her, there she was, hands folded in her lap, ice-cool, spotless. 'My body is a temple, Daniel,' she said, quite kindly. 'When we're married, I'll give you the keys.'

From the top of the next field, the unhappy Kevin saw them sitting like that, and scowled. 'So you're at it too, are you? Well, bloody hell, I'll show you. I'll show you too. Just you wait.'

Chapter 11

'And so now finally as those golden gates have closed behind me, like dozens of other eager, bright-eyed young men, I must step out into the world not knowing (for which of us *can* know?) what the future may hold . . .'

Joseph paused and looked out of the window. Celia and Amos were engaged in a struggle; Celia would hold his hand, Amos did not want it held; while Rose looked passively on. What the future held did not bear thinking about. He went on with his letter. 'So do not be surprised, dearest mama, if for a few weeks, you do not hear from me. Your little lad must find his own feet, must carve out his destiny for himself. This is always a painful process, and one which . . .'

His biro had started to run out. It occurred to him that he could not afford to buy a new one and so would have to steal someone else's. Moreover, he had no idea how to finish the sentence he had just started. One which, one which . . .

The sentence was like his own life. Where would it go? Where could it go!

Celia, meanwhile, still holding the struggling Amos, had arrived at Mrs Woosnam's house. 'Would you mind, just for an hour or so; they get so stroppy in the supermarket, and Hunter's asked me to get . . .'

Mrs Woosnam was, or could be, a kindly soul. 'Just you

leave them with me. They'll be no trouble at all, will you, my lovelies?'

Celia was not aware of the person, who, jacket collar turned up like a spy in a bad film, followed her in the shady recesses of the lane. Soon, she got into her little red car and was off, up the track into the hills.

She found Jamie full of plans. The following week, he was going to London for his interview and hoped to be able to move into the Muswell Hill House as well. Now, they must secretly fix a date, a few weeks away, when Celia and the children would go to Llanafon on the pretext of a dentist appointment; there she would leave the car at the station, catch the afternoon train to Paddington where Jamie would meet her. At first, she would tell the children only that they were going on a holiday; the truth could come later. Then she could think about a divorce, or at least a legal separation.

Thus their new life would begin, simple, free and loving, in Muswell Hill.

Jamie spoke of it with such calm confidence that she could not but share it. He settled her worries about the children, about money, about Hunter. 'It won't go wrong, my darling. How can it?'

The world could be changed, its darkness lifted, its inflexibilities made flexible. You could write your own words on its sands. When Jamie held her in his arms, there was nothing that was not possible.

'Where you off to, then?' said Kevin, looking down from the Land Rover.

'Oh, you know,' said Daniel, vaguely. 'Just a walk, up into the hills. I wondered if I might scrounge a lift.'

'You're a glutton for it, aren't you? Go on then, up you get.' The courtesies of the countryside died hard.

'Thanks very much.'

'Anywhere special in mind?'

'Well, I thought actually, I might have a go at that cave.'

'You lot've got a thing about that bloody cave.'

'I've heard,' said Daniel, carefully, 'there's a rare sort of lichen that grows there.' His new-found purpose had developed in him a strange wiliness. In order to do what he was going to do, he had had to block off certain principles of human behaviour that he had learned from the Professors. The thing was not to be distracted from the purpose. It was easy to know the difference between Right and Wrong, said Anita. She had tried to describe it to him, and now when he thought about it, he could see Right as shining, glorious and white, while Wrong crawled slimily in the gutters. If God had not intended Daniel to do what he had set out to do, He would not have placed Kevin and the Land Rover so conveniently in the way.

'Lichen!' said Kevin. He knew when a person was up to something and had his own ideas about what Daniel might be up to. 'Off we go then. Let's find this bloody lichen!'

They passed the journey pleasantly enough slagging off Dorothy.

'Bloody little tart, is what I think of her.' That was Kevin.

'She doesn't have much in the way of morals, certainly.' Daniel, schooled by Anita, modified his language.

'She'll come to a sticky end, leading men on the way she does.'

'I'm afraid she will,' Daniel said piously, and both were silent as they meditated happily on the kind of sticky end to which Dorothy might come.

But then they saw something that made Kevin stop. 'Hey. Whose bike is that? Belongs to Jamie the vicar's son, don't it? Daft place to bloody leave it.'

'Not so daft when you think. Maybe I'll get out and walk now, Kevin, thank you.'

For before he left the house, Daniel had studied the maps carefully. He knew that the rocky outcrop he could just see on the horizon must be, at last, the cave.

'Suit yourself,' Kevin said, and Daniel got out and began to track through the bracken. The new growth was dense and springy and was far harder to walk through than it looked; it was almost like wading through deep water. He did not realize until he had gone some way that he was not alone. Kevin had parked the Land Rover and was following him.

'Most people take the path,' said Kevin. 'Trust you to go through the bloody middle.'

'I didn't see a path,' Daniel said with dignity. 'What are you doing here?'

'Same as you. Looking for a nice bit of lichen.'

'Eh?'

'Lichen. What you was looking for, or have you forgotten?'

'Oh. Course I haven't forgotten. But . . . I'm not sure you'll really be interested.'

'Rubbish. Nothing like it. Whenever I get a bit fed up, I say to myself, what about a nice bit of lichen? Come on, pull the other one. It's not lichen you're looking for, is it? You must take me for a right . . . You think there's someone there, in that cave, don't you?'

'I really don't know what you're talking about, Kevin.'

'I may look daft, but I'm not. You're on your way to catch someone, aren't you?'

Daniel suddenly felt frightened. 'I don't know. Perhaps I'd better go back.'

'What? Now you've come all this way? 'Sides, wouldn't you like to have a witness?'

'Kevin, look, I . . .'

'Well, why not? We'd both like to see her taught a lesson, like, wouldn't we?'

'What? Oh, all right. And don't make so much noise.'

'Look who's talking,' said Kevin, but he moved quietly through the bracken.

In the distance, they could see the strange humped shape

of rock which was the cave. Dappled with lichen, chrome yellow and burnt orange, it made a vivid contrast with the blue of the sky as the hill swept up to it. The rock was skirted by slopes of scree, but a path of bright green grass led up to it and a thick growth of bracken partly screened the entrance, which could now be seen; a low, black mouth in the rock. Everything was quiet and peaceful. For a moment Daniel saw the world as he would not see it again.

He and Kevin moved forward stealthily, like children playing war. The bracken came to an end and they went on through low, spiny furze and crimson-leaved bilberry. The air was sour with sheep's urine; Kevin wrinkled his nose, but said nothing. At the foot of the slope, Daniel instinctively fell back. For a moment, he remembered the saint, and then he forgot her. The slope led up before him and its tumble of rocky boulders against the bright sky made it look like a ruined castle. He could hear Kevin's breathing, slightly hoarse and strained. A bird — what kind of bird? — hovered in the air.

Then Kevin stopped and gestured for silence. They could hear a sound above them, a strange moaning, gasping sound, like the call of a hunted animal, or the ebb and flow of a storm wind; but it was a human sound. It was a remote, a private, a mysterious sound.

With exaggerated delicacy, Kevin crept forward those last few yards. Before the cave the ground flattened out and made a little apron. He came to a standstill, peering into the cave mouth, and then froze. Daniel, who had momentarily forgotten what he had come looking for, wondered what on earth had made Kevin look so shocked. 'Bloody hell!' he heard Kevin say, softly, and then he, too, stood there and saw what Kevin had seen, in the cave.

Neither of them said anything, not until they had got back to the Land Rover. Kevin pulled out a packet of cigarettes and leaned against the door. Daniel's heart was beating hard. All he could think of saying was, 'At least I don't think they saw us.'

'Wouldn't have seen anything, rate they was at it,' Kevin said hoarsely. 'Bloody hell!'

'Shall we go back home now?'

'Blimey, they was going at it like . . .'

'Kevin, perhaps we'd better . . .'

'You wouldn't think she had it in her. Woman of her age! Blimey! And him too! Bloody vicar's son, *Mistah* Loftus! Bloody University and nose in the air, going at it like . . .'

'Shall we . . .?'

'Well, it only goes to show, don't it? Shows you, just because you got your nose in the air and a posh voice! But, blimey, *her*! No tits and a face like the back of a bus! Blimey. Last person you'd . . .' He stopped and gave Daniel an odd look. 'Hang on a minute. You said it was Dorothy.'

'I never.'

'Yes, you bloody did. You told me it was Dorothy we was after.'

'I didn't. You thought Dorothy.'

'Did you *know* it was going to be Mrs bloody Hunter having it off?'

'No. I mean, yes. I mean, not exactly.'

'You dragged me all the way up here . . . why? Why did you come up here?'

'That's my business,' Daniel said. He was starting to feel better now.

'You knew it was Mrs Hunter. You knew she was having it off with the bloody vicar's son and you wanted to *spy* on her.'

'Not *spy*.'

'What do you call it then?'

'Never you mind.'

'You came to spy on her. You came to spy on Mrs Hunter!' Kevin gave him an odd look.

'Well, why did you come then?'

'That's different.'

'No it's not. You thought it was Dorothy. Why did you want to spy on Dorothy?'

'Because young Dorothy's led me up a right garden path, that's what. If I could catch her, up to a bit of no good, well, all right. I thought that's what you were after too.'

'*Dorothy*?' Daniel looked at Kevin as though he had never even noticed Dorothy's existence.

'Well, she's led us both on, hasn't she? Fair enough, wanting to get an eyeful of Dorothy having it off. But Mrs Hunter . . .'

'I told you. That's my business.'

'Well, it's bloody peculiar, if you ask me. Bloody Peeping Tom. And I'll tell you something else. You can walk back, you can. You can walk all the way down, on your bloody own!'

Daniel tried to be dignified, though it was difficult over the noise of the Land Rover. 'Thank you very much. I'd rather walk, anyway!'

Chapter 12

If . . .

If Celia had looked at Daniel that evening at supper and observed how he scowled and chewed air and ground his hands together and avoided her gaze, she might have realized . . .

And if there and then, on this wisp of suspicion, she had grabbed her children and fled with her lover into the night, like Porphyro and Madeline . . .

Or taken Daniel aside and talked to him gently, for he was not yet quite all Anita's; if she had not been so distracted since his arrival (for although Hunter walked off with the glory, it was usually Celia who sat up through painful nights with white-faced ruined little rich kids, junkies, anorexics and failed suicides, coaxing them back into humanity), if she had only tried to listen to Daniel . . .

If, if, if . . .

But she had done none of these things and now Daniel, for a hotch-potch of reasons, had become her enemy, and even now, in the cliché of enmity, was, over beefburgers and chips, plotting her downfall . . .

At the head of the table, Hunter sat, smiling. St Rhuna's day was to be his day. His spirit had moved upon the face of the waters and had summoned up journalists, photographers, the person from Woman's Hour and a folk group with a Welsh Arts Council grant. At his bidding, prayers would be said, ancient magic fanned into life, music played and bonfires sent flaring against the night sky. Contemplating such things, it was not surprising that he noticed neither Daniel's unease, nor Celia's distraction.

Only Joseph tried to keep conversation afloat that evening.

'Alas, I will be most sad to depart, but duty calls!'

'A pity you can't stay a couple more days, then you'd be here for the ceremony,' Hunter said kindly.

'It cannot be done, my dear Hunter. I must in this case put my own ceremony first. Tomorrow, I shall assemble all my belongings and the morning of St Rhuna's day will find me sadly making my way to dear Llanafon.' The important thing, in fact, was to put as much distance as possible between himself and St Rhuna's, before Hunter tried to bank his cheque.

'I'm afraid I won't have time to take you to the station,' said Hunter. 'Though perhaps Celia . . .'

'Oh, please don't worry about that,' Joseph said. 'I have already been promised a lift.' In fact, since he could not afford the fare, he had no idea of going anywhere near the station. A succession of kindly lorry drivers en route for London, Liverpool or Birmingham was what he hoped for.

'What is this ceremony you have to go back for, anyway?' said Dorothy, suddenly coming to life across the table.

'Oh,' Joseph said modestly, 'I'm sure no one is interested in such things.'

But Hunter smiled in encouragement. 'Yes, do tell us more, Joseph. You're being very cagey about what it is you've been summoned back for.'

'One thing is for certain,' said Joseph, trying to sound mysterious, 'I shall not come out from that clearing in the palm grove the same Joseph that went in.' There had been a book in his school called *Customs Of The Gold Coast*. With its dingy black and white illustrations printed on coarse

122

yellow paper, he had never taken much notice of it and so was ill-versed in the customs of his own country; instead, the book that had ravished his childhood was called *Our Empire Story*, with an embossed cover, gold tooling and full colour illustrations. Here, he had watched with Robert the Bruce in his spidery cave, gone into battle with the Black Prince, loaded cannon against the Don, stormed the heights of Quebec, cradled the dying Nelson in his arms.

It meant he was at a loss to know how to deal with Hunter's question and he tried to dredge from his memory a story that would satisfy. 'The gathering of the princes,' he began, tentatively, 'happens only once every fifty years, but when it does, the call goes out to all the corners of the globe, and it must be obeyed . . .'

Dorothy gave a stifled snort into her beefburgers and Hunter turned to her sharply. 'Dorothy! Apologize to Joseph at once!'

Joseph tried out the voice of Nurse Cavell. 'There is nothing to forgive,' he said.

Such things were lost on Dorothy. Her school history book was called *From Marx To The Mahatma; Twentieth-Century Perspectives*. 'Daniel, if you don't want your chips, can I finish them?'

'You'd do better to finish your beefburger,' Hunter said. 'You waste far too much good food, my girl.'

'God only knows what they put in those things, especially the cheap ones Celia buys.'

'Aren't they any good?' Celia said apologetically. 'They were on special offer.' Tonight, she seemed so absent as to be almost transparent. Daniel stared at her with dislike and shock, trying to reconcile this phantom with what he had glimpsed in the darkness of the cave. What did Celia know? And why could he not know it, too?

'Can I have them?'

'What?'

'Your chips of course, silly.'

'Oh, yes.'

'The human body needs protein,' Hunter said. 'Cells have to be regenerated and although I know it's smart among you young ones to be vegetarian . . .'

'I'm not vegetarian, I just can't bear this rubbish. Ketchup, please.'

'If you think those beefburgers are rubbish, then what do you think goes into that ketchup bottle? Probably enough chemicals to start a bomb factory.'

Dorothy ignored this. 'What about your mother?' she said to Daniel. 'I bet she doesn't give you rotten beefburgers.'

Daniel, taken aback, blinked. 'She's German, actually,' he said irrelevantly.

'Has everyone finished?' said Celia.

'Celia, that was, as always, delicious,' said Joseph. And I, as always, he thought, am lying.

'I'm afraid I didn't have time to make a pudding, but there are tinned oranges.'

'Tinned oranges!' said Hunter benevolently. 'My dear Celia, how you have sinned!'

She glanced up in alarm at the word sin. 'How?'

'You have sinned against the precept of the venerable Dorothy. Thou shalt not eat of tinned oranges, nor of anything that is frozen, or processed or convenient.' Hunter's prejudices had been collected in an earlier generation; food faddism was not amongst them.

'Rubbish,' said Dorothy. 'I love tinned oranges.'

'To put the orange in a tin,' mused Joseph. 'What a strange concept that is for we Africans!'

'You don't grow oranges in Ghana,' Dorothy said.

'Indeed we do. Delicious oranges.'

'No, you don't. You grow cocoa in Ghana. I did it in geography.'

'Cocoa. And oranges, and indeed many things.'

'Oranges come from Spain, California and Israel. Oh,

124

and South Africa, but they're naughty ones. You never see oranges from Ghana.'

Joseph opened his mouth to protest, but shut it again. After all, who was he to defend the truth?

Later that evening, Celia, alerted by a cry, went upstairs to find Charlie sitting up in bed, the traces of tears still on his cheeks. 'Mummy, I was having an evening-mare.' Charlie, unlike others at Disserth House, believed in scrupulous accuracy of description.

Celia held the warm body next to hers. The top of his head smelt warm and very faintly of milk and dirt. That morning, she had held a man in her arms and planned to give up all on his account.

'What did you dream, my love?'

'There was a dark hole and it moved. And I called out and I couldn't find you.'

'I'm here now, my darling.'

'But you weren't there in my dream. I called and called,' he said with only a trace of indignation.

'But you see, I did hear you, in the end.'

He snuggled against her. 'I'm all right now, Mummy, but can you stay, just for a bit, in case the dream comes back?'

'I won't let it come back,' she said, knowing it to be true. Over no one else, not even Jamie, did she have such powers.

Yet even Charlie would only be briefly hers; the lovely child was given to her in temporary ransom for another Charlie; an ungainly youth with spots, who would drink too much and crack dirty jokes with his friends. Ultimately he would leave her for someone else, whom he would love more than he loved his mother. Charlie, more truly hers than anyone else, was not to be hers for ever, and he would not even be the same person as the years went by. Innocence went, never to return, and in retrospect, you could see that it had not been innocence at all, only ignorance. Ignorance was not charming. It had nothing to recommend it. Yet you could not hold Charlie, in all his fragile beauty, his silky hair, his petal-soft skin, his unclouded gaze, without believing in it.

Which was the real Charlie, this one, or the coarsened Charlie that lay in wait?

What cruel tricks the world would play on Charlie. Perhaps it would be better for him to lose his innocence now, as quickly and harshly as possible, that having suffered once, he would suffer no more.

The Professors in Ealing sat down to a meal that was not beefburgers and chips — there was a soufflé of parmesan cheese and a chicory salad, but there was no happiness. Daniel had just sent another letter home.

'But now he is talking of marriage to this girl!' said Daniel's mother.

'Stupid lad! He doesn't mean it.'

'Daniel does not say things he does not mean. Frank, he is still a child.'

'Every mother thinks that about her son.'

'Darling, do not patronize me, please.'

'If you want a problem to solve, apply yourself to poor old Geoffrey. Twelve hours of tapes to transcribe and not a soul this side of the world who can be found to speak the language!'

'Then it becomes a problem for the School of Oriental and African Studies to solve. I really do not see that it's such a difficulty.'

'Oh, we've tried SOAS. Seems the last bloke there who could have done the job was squeezed out in the cuts. Of course, he went off to Harvard; doing very nicely for himself, so I hear, but it means poor old Geoffrey has a brilliant piece of research all tied up in gobbledygook.'

'Sometimes, I wonder whether it is a man I am married to, or a word processor. It is my son I am worried about, not some bloody Nigerian tapes.'

So unusual was it for his wife to swear that Daniel's father looked up in mild surprise. 'Not Nigerian,' he said. 'He did the research in . . .'

'I am not interested in where he did the research! Daniel is in Wales, and he is in trouble!'

'Daniel is in a vulnerable state of mind. Look, how much longer is he booked to stay in this place?'

'A week, two weeks more.'

'Well then, let it run its course. He'll have a good rest, come back to London, settle down and forget all about this girl.'

'So you say, but I can't feel so hopeful. There's something about this situation that worries me. Daniel is not like other boys of his age.'

'And a good thing too, if you ask me. Now have another glass of wine and stop fretting.'

'But I think this has always been our trouble. Just because he shows no interest in girls, stays in his room at night and reads his books, just because it is convenient and we are selfish, we think, jolly good show, he is not like other chaps.'

'Do you know, I had a student in the other day — Collins — father's a headmaster too — who had no idea Henry James was American. In line for a 2:1, too. God only knows what they teach them in the schools these days, because I don't.'

'Frank, you are not listening to me!'

'I'm listening, my dear; but I honestly think you're making a mountain out of a molehill.'

'A mountain out of a molehill! A storm in a teacup! How comfortable your English clichés are! Just say anything rather than have to act!'

Daniel's father looked at her. He knew, as he knew the world was round, that in the end, reason would prevail and Daniel must come to his senses, but it grieved him to see his wife upset. 'Listen, if you feel so strongly, then why not go up there and drag him home early. Perhaps this chap Hunter's not all he's cracked up to be. Well, in that case, we remove Daniel from his clutches and no harm done.'

'I could leave after breakfast,' mused Daniel's mother.

'I'd come with you, of course, but what with scripts pouring in and this meeting tomorrow, it just isn't on. Of course, if it were a matter of life and death . . .'

'A matter of life and death! Well, I think, perhaps, it may be a matter of life. Does that count as the same thing?'

That night, Celia, as she prepared for bed, felt as she often did that she was not one Celia but a hundred Celias, seen in an infinitely vanishing perspective of mirrors, each Celia trapped and tiny and helpless. Only by seeing herself through Jamie's eyes could she see a whole person, clear and beautiful.

Why could Jamie be firm and clear where she was not? Was it simply that she was older, and knew more? Was she so much weaker than he? Or was it simply that there was no such person as Celia, and that even Jamie's image of her was a chimera?

Yet even as she formulated this thought, another part of her brain cried out in revolt against it. She was real and if it was only in Jamie's loving arms that she felt so, then it was to Jamie that she must cling, at no matter what cost.

Of Hunter's identity there could be no doubt. Big, strong and steady, he pulled his white T-shirt over his head and shoulders and unzipped his trousers. The world needed Hunters. It could not have ticked over these millions of years if it had been peopled only by uncertain Celias, however much nicer they might be. 'Have you seen my blue pyjamas, darling?' Naked, he stood before her, firm-bellied, strong-thighed and broad-chested, crowned by the white halo of hair and beard; his genitals nestling confidently in their place, the mark of his manhood, which had penetrated her as a man puts a key only in his own front door and made her his. Their marriage was as real as could be. One flesh. Celia and John. Mr and Mrs. As long as they both should live.

'I'm sorry, darling, the blue ones are in the wash.' The endearment came automatically.

'Not to worry,' Hunter said mildly. 'I'll wear the others. Get them for me, will you? I can't wander about like this.'

'Of course,' she said. They were outside in the airing cupboard, and she found them, warm and clean, washed and ironed by her.

'There's a good girl,' he said, as he took them from her, while she averted her eyes from that big, confident, assertive frame. He was a monument, a colossus.

That night, he was in benevolent mood. 'Are you going to come to bed, Celia,' he said, propped among pillows, Jove framed by white clouds, 'or do you intend to scrub the floor as well?' For reluctant to join him, she was pottering around the bedroom, folding clothes and arranging ornaments.

The only thing that seemed to be worrying him was the weather. A bad day on the morrow might ruin his ceremony. 'I hope it won't rain,' he said, 'but you just can't tell. There were some ominous clouds this evening.'

'Oh, I'm sure it won't rain,' she said.

'You'll see to it personally, will you Celia? Do come to bed, love. You're making me nervous.'

'Just let me find my cotton wool.' She felt like Delilah.

'Little Celia,' he said, suddenly and tenderly. 'You're looking very pretty these days, you know that?'

'Oh!' she said, disconcerted. 'No, I'm not, I'm sure I can't be.'

'And still you jump like a startled rabbit every time somebody pays you a compliment, don't you, my little one?'

'No, I don't, I mean I . . .'

'Stop talking rubbish and come to bed.' He smiled and held out his arms and she remembered how that very firmness, that monumental quality had once attracted her. 'Little Celia!' he repeated gently.

Quite clearly, tonight Hunter was going to be nice. And this was how things become complicated. For whereas in Jamie's eyes Hunter was nothing but an absolute monster, she knew him to be only a monster some of the time. And even his monstrosity, when you examined it, could dissolve or spread out into things that were really not monstrous at all.

She turned out the light and climbed in beside him. A touch from him must set all her nerves screaming and jangling, but tonight, it seemed, he did not want to make love to her. His ceremony was the big thing now, and he could think of nothing else.

'The problem, of course, may be Loftus,' he said, and she was filled with horror, but it was all right, he was simply talking about the vicar. 'He does his best, of course, but I know that in his heart of hearts, he thinks the whole thing's a bit pagan. I wonder whether he'll manage to convey that. The Woman's Hour girl might want to interview him, and I don't think he'd handle that at all well.'

She lay, rigid, beside him. 'Now you've arranged everything with Anita, haven't you?' he went on. 'I hope there'll be enough food. The band should be all right. Tim Lockwood speaks highly of them . . .'

He talked and talked, and soon, he slept.

She did not. The hours of night began to pass, slowly, each minute measured and endured, in darkness and silence.

Chapter 13

By the following morning, the sky had filled with clouds. As Daniel looked through the dripping creeper that framed his window, he could see them, dull metallic grey and soft, spongy white, massed in heaps from the horizon, like another line of hills. But there were also uneven patches of sky, delphinium blue, and the early morning sun shone with glittering intensity. The garden quivered and vibrated under the odd mixed light. Joseph came into his room without knocking.

'*So foul and fair a day I have not seen,*' he said. 'Daniel, I come to say farewell.'

'Oh, I'm sorry,' Daniel said, and meant it, for, though he had never liked Joseph very much, if he went something familiar would go with him. Disserth House had come to feel, if not like home, at least a place whose inhabitants he had become used to.

'*Parting,*' went on Joseph, who was in quoting mood, '*is*, is it not, *so sweet a sorrow.*'

'Such.'

'I beg your pardon?'

'*Such sweet sorrow.* You've got it wrong. Like fresh fields and pastures new and all that.'

'Ah, yes. You take the words from my mouth. I go to fresh fields and pastures new.'

'But it isn't,' said Daniel helplessly. 'That's what every-one thinks, but it isn't. It's *woods*.'

'Then it is to fresh fields and woods that I go. How well the poet expresses such things for us.'

'He might, if you gave him a chance,' muttered Daniel. There might be worse things than misquotation, in fact there were, adultery as he now knew, being one of them, but there was nothing like a person getting a quotation wrong for making you really angry.

'So farewell, Daniel,' Joseph said. 'Perhaps we may meet again some day, far from the maddening crowd.'

The door closed behind him. Really, anybody other than Joseph and you'd suspect he was doing it on purpose.

Kevin had told Robert Evans from the Bryn. Robert told his sister, Clare. Clare told young Mrs Rees from Pentwyn. Young Mrs Rees told Mrs Woosnam. The chances were that sooner or later, the news would have reached Hunter's ears anyhow.

But at ten precisely, Anita arrived in a pretty lemon yellow dress with broderie anglaise at the neck and bodice. She wore matching sandals and her hair, newly washed, shone with golden highlights.

Celia was out, with the children. Hunter was in his study. 'I've got to talk to you,' hissed Daniel. Anita gave him a look, grave and yet comprehending, as though she had already taken in his discovery and knew what to do about it. At such moments, she assumed a stern, superhuman air, a statue on a granite plinth. He felt better already.

He followed her into the kitchen, where she scrubbed down the kitchen table, and then, like a surgeon preparing for an operation, laid out everything she was going to need, neatly marshalling spring onions, lettuce, tomatoes, radishes. With a sharp little knife she began to slice bridge rolls, first a deep cut to the soft heart, then a quick slash from side to side. Then she passed them to Daniel. 'You

132

may as well butter these for me,' she said, 'while you tell me about it.'

He watched the swift movements of her little white hands; how deftly they sliced shining red and white disks from a radish, or plunged into tomatoes soft as flesh, or hard, glittering onions. 'Well, Daniel?'

How to begin, confronting such skill? 'I went up the hill after her. Kevin gave me a lift. We went up, and we saw this bike, hidden. I think it was *his*, you know. Kevin stopped the Land Rover, and then he said, wait a minute, I'm coming with you, so he did.' Daniel stopped. He knew this was no way to structure a narrative and his mother would have said, 'Be more precise. Tell everything carefully in order.'

But this didn't seem to worry Anita. In fact she smiled and said, 'You're doing fine, Daniel. What happened next?'

Oh, goodness. For it had never occurred to him that the bit that followed was going to be put into words, *could* be put into words.

'Go on, Daniel,' she said, gently encouraging.

'We saw . . .'

'Yes?'

'Look, Anita, I'd rather not . . .'

'I know it's difficult, Daniel.'

'Yes, it is. Jolly difficult.' He sat down and began to eat a radish.

'Don't eat them, Daniel, they don't belong to us. And we must carry on working while we talk. We have no business to waste Mr Hunter's time. Right. So you saw Jamie Loftus's bicycle, and you went up the hill with Kevin . . .'

Daniel took a deep breath. He got himself and Kevin as far as the cave, listening to the noises which came from within, then he stopped.

'Yes?' Anita was now flicking slivers of cheese on to rolls.

'Can't you guess?' he said sheepishly, as small children do.

133

'You have to tell me. There must be no mistake about this.'

'Well, they were in there.'

'*Who* were, Daniel?'

'*They* were. Jamie Loftus. And her. Mrs Hunter. Celia.'

'And what were they doing in the cave?' Her voice was as sharp as the knife with which she now sliced tomatoes. 'You have to tell me, Daniel. And do stop tearing that piece of bread to bits.'

'They were . . . they were . . .' He put the bits of bread on the table, '. . . *doing it.*'

'Are you trying to tell me they were engaging in fornication?'

Was he? Well, probably. 'Yes.'

'You're quite sure of that?'

'Yes.'

'Clothes had been taken off?'

'Yes, I suppose . . .'

'You *suppose*?' It was like being in a court of law. 'Which clothes?'

'The usual clothes. Look, Anita, is this necessary?'

'Sorry, Daniel, I'm afraid it is. You're quite sure that the couple performing this . . . this disgusting act were Mrs Hunter and the vicar's son?'

'Kevin recognized them too,' Daniel said in desperation. 'He knew who it was, because he thought it was Dorothy. We talked about it, ask him.'

'I have no intention of doing any such thing. Your word is sufficient for me.'

Daniel breathed a sigh of relief. A giggle threatened to rise in his throat and he turned it into a cough.

'Poor Daniel. You've done a very good day's work. Have a glass of water.'

'Is it? A good day's work, I mean?'

'Of course. Far better for everyone that this dreadful thing come to light now.'

'What are you going to do now?'

She gave him a look of surprise. 'Do you really need to ask me that, Daniel? There's only one thing we can do. I hope we're in no doubt about that. Now, please could I ask you to pass me the salad cream?'

In the graveyard, Mrs Potter tried to weave white roses among marguerite daisies, but the roses would not twine and the daisies kept dropping petals. Her husband had constructed an arch out of chicken wire, and Mr Hunter had described the effect he wanted her to produce; like flowers falling from heaven. They must cover the arch and lie in a luxuriant tumble at the base, white interspersed with blood-red blooms (virgin and martyr). Instead, there was too much chicken wire and only a smallish untidy heap of roses. Part of the trouble was that there were simply not enough white roses in the village to produce the effect. What about a nice Whiskey Mac, she said to Hunter, I've got plenty of those. But Hunter was adamant; snow-white and blood-red it had to be; nothing else would do.

When she saw Mrs Woosnam coming across the grave-yard, she called out to her, 'Help!' But Mrs Woosnam's face was anxious. 'I don't know whether I ought to say,' she said, sitting down heavily on the grass bank behind the well, 'but I've heard the most dreadful story.'

At once Mrs Potter saw that she was in for something more interesting than white roses. 'Tell me all about it.'

Mrs Woosnam took a deep breath. 'Well,' she said. 'You don't like to gossip, do you?'

Hunter was busy. 'Not now, dear, if you don't mind,' he had said several times in answer to Anita's request. However, she persisted, and in the end, Daniel watched the study door closing on the pair of them.

But he and Anita had talked of something else that morning as they buttered the bridge rolls, and it was this that now absorbed most of his attention as he went upstairs and began to pack.

While still in his bedroom, he heard a knock and went to open the door, expecting Anita. It was Celia.

'Everyone seems to have vanished,' she said, laughing, 'and I need a big strong man to help me.'

Daniel opened his mouth and he tried to think of excuses, but none sprang to mind, so he followed her downstairs.

As he stepped into the hall, he saw Hunter's study door open and out came Anita. Her face was impassive; he could read nothing there. For a moment, all three of them stood in the hallway, Celia, Daniel, Anita. Celia said, 'Hallo, Anita!' in what was, for her, a quite animated fashion, and Anita replied steadily, 'Good morning, Mrs Hunter.'

'Mrs Hunter . . . er . . . wants me to help her,' Daniel muttered.

'Oh, I'm sorry,' said Celia. 'Did you have other plans?'

'It's all right, Mrs Hunter, it can wait. Daniel, I'll see you later, as we agreed.'

He gave her a look of panic; was she really going to leave him like this? Hunter's study door was shut, and there was no knowing what had passed behind it. 'Take your time, Daniel,' Anita said. 'I'll wait for you.'

There was nothing for it but to follow Celia out into the yard where she had parked the car; she wanted someone to carry sacks of chicken feed into the shed near the vegetable garden. The children, squabbling, ran around them. 'Oh, Daniel, you are kind,' Celia said, as he swung a sack on to his shoulder. 'We have to buy this stuff in bulk,' she continued, 'and this morning was the only time I could collect it.' Celia had also used the garden centre phone to talk briefly to Jamie — neither Deirdre nor Norman were about, and they had tentatively fixed a day for their flight. Then he had whispered things to her, such loving, secret and intimate things that she was flooded with joy. Now she even felt sorry for Daniel in his awkwardness. 'Daniel, we're pleased to have you here, I hope you know that, do you?'

In the little dark shed that smelled of cobwebs, of damp and of sacking, he could say nothing, and she went on. 'I hope you're feeling better. You look much happier than when you arrived.' It was her standard speech for softening hearts and it usually worked; especially when she turned on, as now she did, the gentle warmth which had so captivated Jamie. 'You must have been feeling a bit left out with this St Rhuna's day thing going on, but you haven't grumbled a bit.'

Let her go away, Daniel prayed. Please, just let her go away. The prayer was not answered. She leaned against the doorway and continued talking. 'It's awful, isn't it, when things start going wrong? I do know what it's like.'

What did she know? What had she done? Oh, help, help!

'You know,' she went on, 'you've never really talked about what happened at Cambridge, have you?'

He breathed in the earthy, cool smell and stared at her, framed by the door, gently lit by the garden beyond. In the semi-darkness, seeing her as her lover had seen her, her pallor was soft and glowing, her eyes full of sympathy, her smile irresistible.

''S all right, I mean I don't really . . .' And suddenly, his subconscious released the catch and presented him whole and entire with that last day at Cambridge. He remembered now sitting in the stuffy exam room, writing . . . rubbish. Pages and pages of rubbish! No wonder they had sent him away. He was aware of Amos standing outside, looking at him with dispassionate curiosity, while Celia shooed him away and shut the door on them so they were alone in the loamy darkness. 'I'm all right, really.' But really he wasn't. To his horror, he began to cry. Celia reached out and gently touched his shoulder. 'Let it come,' she said. 'You'll feel better afterwards.'

He, Daniel Green, had cracked up! He had written

137

rubbish. Something had snapped and he had not been able to go on. And the odd thing was, that the knowledge had been there all the time, but he had never taken it out and looked at it. Now things fell into place. For a few moments, he quite forgot the thing he and Anita had just visited upon Celia. Celia was standing there in the darkness and she was kind. Her kindness was overwhelming. Now the words rushed from him. 'My parents, they were so . . . so bloody good and kind and they expected so much, they just took it for granted that I was clever, you see, just like they were, and I knew, at least I didn't know really, not until I sat down to do that exam, that I wasn't at all, I mean I could remember things and pass tests, but that's not being clever, is it, but they were always so good, oh God, I hate them, no, that's not true. I don't hate them. But they don't understand. When I saw that paper, I wanted, I really wanted . . .'

'Yes Daniel?'

'I wanted to hurt them and do badly. I'd had enough. I'd just had enough . . .' He slowly decelerated and stood looking at her.

'There now. You'll feel better with it all out of your system.'

Oh, when Celia wanted to be nice! Normally, her quiet glow was quite eclipsed by Hunter's great neon beam, but when Celia wanted to be, she was quite irresistible. In the darkness of the shed, he looked at her as a dog looks at its master. 'I'm sorry we've never managed to have a talk before,' she said, 'but everything's been so busy.' Daniel shuffled his feet and sniffed. A great sob came up from his chest and broke from him with a shudder. But he did feel better. The tears had washed everything out of him. Celia's hair and face were suffused by the light that filtered through the dingy window, transforming her. She was all love, all kindness, all goodness. Daniel remembered that someone . . . who was it? . . . loved her. Perhaps it was himself. He loved her. That was it.

But then, in a brisk everyday voice, she said, 'Well, I must be getting along. Heaven knows what Amos is up to,' and he remembered, as the door opened and the dim saintly light was replaced by the common indifferent glare outside, that he did not love her. He remembered, too, then and only then, his treachery.

Chapter 14

Yet barely twenty minutes later, there he was, in the little car Anita had borrowed, speeding through the countryside. He had not seen Celia again when he collected his suitcase from the house, and Hunter's door remained firmly shut, with only Amos to ambush him by the stairs. 'Where are you going, Hanky-panky-wanky?'

Something had happened to Daniel; he was aware that it was important, but by the time he had reached the front door with his suitcase, he knew it was something he had to kill quickly. Soon, he had nearly succeeded in doing so. Over and over, he said to himself, 'She had it coming to her. It's none of my business. It's not my fault, not my fault, not my fault.'

He said it to Anita, self-righteously. 'It's not my fault.'

'No, of course it isn't,' she soothed. 'No one will blame you. Now you did remember everything, didn't you?'

'I think so.'

'Because you don't want to leave anything there, do you? We want to put Disserth House and all that it stands for behind us.' ('I'm sorry,' Celia had said to Anita, 'I'm afraid I must tell you that I shan't be needing you any more.' 'That's quite all right,' Anita replied coldly, 'I was intending to leave anyway,' and Celia, too wrapped up in her own concerns, noticed nothing, thinking merely that she had got away with what might have been a sticky scene.)

'But what did Hunter *say* Anita?'

'There are some things,' she said, turning the wheel sharply to avoid a ditch, 'that perhaps we shouldn't talk about.'

'Yes, I know that, but I just wondered, was he angry when you told him, or what?'

'It wasn't a pleasant experience, as I'm sure you can imagine. Oh, you nasty man!' This was addressed, not to Daniel, but to a Volvo driver who had hooted, having narrowly missed her on a sharp bend. 'I don't know why everyone has to be in such a hurry,' she added.

'But Hunter must have said something!' he persisted.

She, who had been so demanding of detail from him earlier on, now turned a slightly pained face upon him. 'Indeed he did, Daniel. But there are things that it's best not to speak of, don't you think?'

'Yes,' he said mutinously. For a moment, his loyalty to Anita wavered. He thought of Celia smiling at him in the darkness and just at that minute he would have given anything to have been there in the shed with her. But then, usefully for Anita, had she known it, a bit of sexual jealousy raised its mean little head. He remembered what he had seen in the cave and he realized that it wasn't Daniel that Celia wanted, it was Jamie Loftus. He saw again vividly the strange and naked tangle of limbs, heard Celia's cries. 'Dreadful,' he said.

'I beg your pardon?'

'It was dreadful,' he said, 'what those two were getting up to in the cave. I mean doing it like that, where anyone could see you . . . and making all those noises and . . .'

'Yes, dreadful. That's the only word for it.'

'I mean, I know people must do it, but like *that* and with *Loftus*, I mean, he's nothing special, is he, and in the middle of the day, too. I can't imagine what she sees in Jamie Loftus.'

'Adultery is always dreadful,' she said, gently steering his thoughts in the proper direction.

'Oh, yes, I know,' he agreed.

'How anyone can make vows and then break them! It's beyond me. Once I make my vows to someone, it'll be for life. That's the way I am, I can't help it.'

'Me, too,' he said, though with less certainty.

She smiled at him. 'We must never have secrets from each other, you and I.' Bit by bit, she began to reassert her supremacy over his heart.

'No, we mustn't.'

'I'll never treat you like Mrs Hunter treats poor Mr Hunter, you can be sure of that. That's the best present a girl can give the man she loves, don't you think, the keys of the temple? I could never give them to anyone else.'

'I know you wouldn't, Anita.'

Professor Green was in her car too. By lunchtime, she had just reached Gloucester. The historian in her could not help taking in the cathedral, its solid bulk with the astonishing lacy towers rising from the plain, above the terrace streets, the dreary motorway, the dull hunks of modern buildings. When the cathedral was new, that plain would have stretched bleak and empty, and her careful mind automatically set about reconstructing that time, the shrine to Faith in a muddy field, among wooden scaffolding, wicker baskets of rubble, stonemasons clambering like flies, anonymous and expendable, lost in the ultimate certainty of God. Now hellfire and sin and paradise had dwindled into metaphors and with them had gone belief in those ancient virtues; faith and hope and innocence. Innocence! Yet Daniel was innocent, if anyone was, and if innocence was harmless, why should she fear for him so? Innocence could not, could it, cause harm and havoc? It was dangerous to nobody. The innocent was protected; he wore, like Sir Peredur, his purity as a shield to protect him from wild beasts. Daniel could come to no harm; and he could harm nobody.

So anyway the Professor reasoned as the towers of Gloucester cathedral shrank to a mere suggestion of filigree on the horizon behind her.

In his study, Hunter still sat at his desk. In certain moments, all people, monster, saint, coward or hero, are as one.

He sat there stunned, a man abused, betrayed, violated, his world falling apart about him. Yet he was still Hunter. As the initial shock was absorbed, he began to assemble it, slowly, carefully.

'Is there a pub here?' called out the young man from the battered van. He had a fresh, surprised face and a severe prison haircut. The other men in the van were all older, in grubby denims, with beards, granny glasses and balding heads. 'Hippies,' thought Dorothy, contemptuously. But the young bloke was cool. They smiled at each other, travellers meeting in a vast desert.

'Not here. There's one in the next village. Down the road, half a mile, left, then right again.'

One of the men began to sing, loudly, '*Like a bridge over trou-oubled water, I will . . .*'

'Shut up, Bill, will you,' said the boy wearily without much affection. 'Sorry. You'd better tell me again.'

'Down the road . . .'

But the man started up again once more. '*Shut up,*' yelled the boy. Then he grinned at Dorothy. 'Tell you what. I'll never get anywhere with these wallies. Why don't you hop in and you can show us?'

Dorothy considered. 'Yeah, okay. Why not?'

'Great,' said the boy, as the older men hooted and made suggestive comments. 'Look, just shut up, will you? Sorry, I didn't mean you. Hey, we're looking for a guy called Hunter. D'you know him?'

★

143

What Hunter had done, when finally he came out of his study, was to scoop up the children and take them out of the house. 'Come along my lambs,' he said, 'we're going to have a nice walk, and you can have sweets afterwards. Mummy and Daddy have got to have a talk.' Mrs Woosnam was surprised to see them, but, yes, she said, she could certainly have the kiddies for half an hour. She did not say anything else, but she pulled a knowing face as Hunter departed.

Celia, meanwhile, had been drifting around the kitchen, putting finishing touches to the food. She found that the children were not in the living-room, where she had left them, and Hunter's study was empty. This was so unusual a combination of circumstances that she began to be anxious. By the time Hunter returned, she was panicking. When he stood there, huge in the doorway, she had guessed what she was in for.

Anita and Daniel arrived at the Fellowship House just before lunch. At once Daniel was surrounded by kind faces. The story of the moral turpitude which had driven him from Disserth House was enough to secure their warmest sympathies. Daniel could stay there, sharing with one of the boys, of course, for as long as he liked. The hospitality of the House was upheld by mysterious, invisible sources. He would be safe there. They were his friends. Jesus was his extra special friend. Jesus would look after him. Everyone would look after him.

'Sit down, Celia,' Hunter said.

'I think I'd rather stand if you don't mind.'

'Please yourself.' But he sat down, facing her across the desk like an interrogator. His snowy nimbus of hair looked wilder than usual and his eyes had turned steely grey.

Celia decided not to prevaricate. 'I imagine you've found out,' she said. Her voice did not come out as she meant; it sounded light, almost on the verge of giggling. The phone

144

rang. Hunter picked it up. Celia listened to a brief conversation, perfectly courteous. 'Three thirty. Yes. And afterwards in the church hall. Yes, please do. Oh no, not at all. Fine. Splendid. I look forward to seeing you.'

He put the receiver back on the hook, held it there a moment, and then lifted it off, all the time looking Celia hard in the eyes. She could hear the faint whirr of the receiver as he laid it on its side. They were cut off from the world, she and he.

'My God, Celia,' he said at length.

'So how did you find out?' she said, still in the light, unsuitable voice.

'Does it matter?'

'I was going to tell you soon, anyhow.'

He waited a long time before answering. 'Good of you, Celia.' His voice was steady but stretched taut.

'Perhaps it's better like this . . . Hunter, I want to leave you.'

As if he had not heard her, he said, 'How long has this been going on, may I ask?'

'Is that relevant?'

'I think so, yes. I would like to know, you see, just how long you have been cuckolding me.' He spat out the unfamiliar word.

'It isn't like that!'

'Is it not, Celia? Then what is it like? I'd be most grateful if you would enlighten me.' But she did not reply and he had to repeat it. '*How long*?'

'I don't know exactly.'

'You do know, exactly.'

Yes, she did. 'Four weeks.' And three days, and . . . She did not mention the three days.

'And *where* may I ask . . . forgive my curiosity, but I have a strange urge to know . . . just where exactly do you . . . now, how do they put it these days? . . . *have it off*?'

'Oh, for God's sake, Hunter!'

'I'm sorry, do I upset you? How else shall I put it? Fuck, perhaps? Just where do you *fuck*?'

'Hunter, that's not important, I told you . . .'

'But you do fuck, don't you? This hasn't just been, how shall we say, a mere marriage of minds, has it? There has been a certain coming together of a carnal nature, hasn't there?'

'Yes, I suppose so, but . . .'

'You suppose so? Are you uncertain?'

'No, of course not.'

'Then let me hear you.'

'What do you want me to say?'

'You know perfectly well. Has Jamie Loftus fucked you?'

'Hunter, please!'

'Yes or no, Celia?'

'*Yes!*'

'In the back of the car? In a field? Behind the church hall? At the vicarage? Oh, dear I hope not. In our own bed perhaps? That would be a thrill for both of you, wouldn't it?'

'No.'

'Or in the cave, perhaps? St Rhuna's cave to be more precise. Ah. I see I've struck home. Yes. For God's sake, Celia, what a fool you are! Don't you know that in a place like this someone's going to catch you at it sooner or later. And what a fine sight it must have been, my wife and the vicar's son!'

'Hunter! Listen to me. Jamie and I love each other . . .'

'Love!' he said scathingly. 'What can you possibly know of love?'

'Quite a lot, actually. Hunter, listen . . .'

'So much that you'll sacrifice everything you have for it? Your children. Charlie? Amos? Rose? You might care nothing for my feelings, indeed, your actions have shown that you quite clearly don't, but you might have spared a moment to think about *them*. What do you think it will feel like for them to know that their mother is the village slag?'

'This is ridiculous, Hunter, they're far too young to understand. Look, I'm sorry if you're upset . . .'

'Upset?' he said. 'Sorry? Oh, Celia, Celia, how you abuse language!'

'You know I'm not clever with words, like you are. I find it hard to say the things I want.'

'You seemed to find no difficulty saying them to Jamie Loftus. Although I forget, you probably didn't bother *saying* very much, did you? Conversation was decidedly not what you were after.'

'Hunter, I'm trying to tell you, it's not like that . . .'

'So you keep saying. But what it *is* like, you don't seem to have managed to say so far.'

'I love Jamie. Jamie loves me.'

'I see.'

'You don't. How can you? Hunter, I want to leave you.'

There was a pause. 'You love him. I love you. Where, pray, does this leave me?'

'I'm sorry, Hunter, I don't think you do love me. I don't think you ever have.'

'For your sake, have I forsaken all others. I have given you everything it was in my power to give. I have protected you. I have — perhaps you forget — nursed you back from the brink of suicide. You are the mother of my children. I have never, as you know, looked at another woman since I married you. Yet all this, years of love and devotion, counts as nothing, in the face of four weeks and a randy schoolboy!'

'I won't listen to you talking like this! It just isn't true.'

'Jamie Loftus! When you came here, he was still in nappies. Even now, he's hardly got rid of his pimples. Oh, he's really on to a good thing, isn't he? Can you imagine how he describes it to his friends, all the little things you say, all the little things you like him to do . . .'

'Hunter, listen to me . . .'

147

'*Jamie Loftus*! Celia, how could you? Be unfaithful to me if you must, indeed, perhaps you must, perhaps it's in your nature, and I must learn to wear my horns with dignity, but for God's sake, please show some discernment about who you leap into bed with!'

'Hunter, will you stop talking, and just listen!'

Hunter folded his arms across his wide chest and leaned back in his seat. 'I'm listening now. Pray continue.'

'It isn't like what you say. Jamie isn't like that! He may be young, but he isn't . . . we love each other. You can't tell me we don't. You don't understand. You never understand.'

'I never understand. I see. Carry on.'

'You say you love me, but I'm sorry, I just don't believe it. I'm just another of your possessions. And I don't love you. Once I thought I did, or I wouldn't have married you, but I was wrong. I want to leave you. I want to live with Jamie. He wants it too.'

'I see. And where do our children fit into this little scheme? What about Charlie, Amos and Rose? What do they have to say?'

'We'll look after them. I won't abandon them.'

'So as well as taking my wife, this boy also has designs on my children, does he?'

'My children.'

'My children. *Our* children.'

'I couldn't leave the children. You know that.'

'So what do you intend to do with them?'

'We have our plans. They're none of your business.'

'My children,' he said, picking out his words with utmost delicacy, 'they are none of my business, are they?'

'I didn't mean that.'

'Or perhaps you're trying to tell me that they aren't my children anyway. Perhaps this isn't the first summer you've had your knickers off for somebody in St Rhuna's cave?'

'Please don't talk like that.'

'I'm sorry, do I offend you? Celia, let us get one thing straight. The children, *my* children, or so I must hope, are not going. You are not taking the children.'

'I'm not leaving them. I couldn't.'

'You are not taking them.' Each word fell like a splinter of glass.

'You have no right . . .'

'Celia,' he said, 'some years ago, or have you forgotten, you had a session in a mental hospital. So depressed and incapable were you that you tried to do away with yourself. At that time, I played the role of your therapist. Indeed, I have your case notes still, the notes of a mentally sick, unstable woman. And now this same woman is telling me she wants to run off with a twenty-year-old boy. Do you seriously think any court is going to grant you custody of those children?'

'They couldn't take them away from me! I'm their mother.'

'You are their mother just as long as you behave responsibly towards them. In law you are no longer entitled to a mother's rights if you abuse them. Didn't you know that?'

'Nobody could take them away.'

'Celia, if you leave me for this lout, *I* will take them away. Have no fear of that.'

'You couldn't do it.'

'Consider your record, my dear. An abortion at nineteen, a suicide attempt, a spell in the — where was it? the Maudsley, I think. Valium. Good Lord, how you rattled with it when we first met. And then treatment for depression again, was there not, after Amos? Dr Webb in Llanafon must have your notes and your prescriptions.'

'That was just post-natal depression. Everybody gets that.'

'I am merely stating the facts as a judge would see them. Would you give such a woman custody of her children?'

149

'It wouldn't be like that,' she said wildly. 'I can prove that I can look after my children. No one would take them from me if they knew. I love them. I love them far more than you've ever done, for all your clever words. They'll be happy with me, I swear it.'

'Are you saying I don't love my children?'

'Well, look at Dorothy! Look at the way she is now! She can't wait to get away.'

'Celia, you are Dorothy's stepmother. For ten years she has looked to you as the only mother she knows. It has been your job to care for her. And what an influence you prove to be! Celia, what have you done for Dorothy?'

'I've done quite a lot, as you know. But, oh, what's the use? You don't want to listen.'

'That, at any rate, is true,' he said wearily. 'I don't want to listen. I don't want to listen to my wife telling me how she has been deceiving me and how she wants to leave. I would give anything not to have listened to this squalid tale. But it seems there is no choice.'

'I didn't mean to hurt you. I can't say any more than that.'

'Did you not?' he said. 'Did you not? The one day of the year which I had allowed myself to look forward to, my great day when everything that I had worked for here was to come together in one glorious celebration. If you didn't mean to hurt me, Celia, your sense of timing is immaculate.'

'I'm sorry it worked out this way, but I can't help that. Look, this conversation isn't getting us anywhere. I'm going to the kitchen. We can talk later on.'

'No,' he said. 'We talk about it now. You are not leaving me, Celia.'

'I'm sorry, I'm afraid you can't stop me.'

'Can't I? I am, I think a decent man. In return for my decency, I have already been deserted by one wife. But let me tell you, I won't let it happen a second time.'

'But if I want to go,' she said dully, 'you can't stop me.'

He nodded, smiled suddenly, and brought his hands together in what seemed like a gesture of exultation. Then he rose and went to a filing cabinet at the far side of the room. From a drawer, he took out a cardboard file from which he extracted a letter.

'Read this, Celia.'

Bewildered, Celia took the sheet of paper, already discoloured with age. It was dated some years ago.

The letter read thus:

My dear Hunter,

I am most grateful to you for the succour you gave me in my hour of need. For many years this thing has weighed upon me like a stone, and though it is known to my Creator, and I must hope, forgiven by Him, as all things can be forgiven, yet there has also been a need to put things right with my fellow men. The talk we had last night has set my conscience, if not at rest, at least as at much ease as it can ever know after what I did to Robert. God knows I have sinned, but now perhaps I can live with the knowledge of it and spend the rest of my life making amends. I swear to you that nothing like that event will ever happen again. I know I can count on your discretion, Hunter, and that my secret is as safe in your hands as it is in God's . . .'

The shaky signature took her some time to decipher.

'Norman?' she said. 'I don't understand.'

'The Reverend Norman. Our honoured vicar. Your boyfriend's father.'

'But . . .?'

'The day before he wrote this letter, Norman Loftus came to me in deep distress. Something was preying on his mind and he could hardly live with it. Confession was what was needed, but he could not go to his superiors because if he confessed to them, he would probably lose everything.'

'Hunter, I hardly see what this has to do with me.'

'Just bear me out. Well, it seems that the Loftus males find their lusts hard to control. Many years ago, when Norman Loftus was a curate in Manchester, he developed a passion for a young altar boy, the Robert whose name he unwisely mentions. The passion was ultimately consummated. That is, he seduced the boy.'

'Hunter, I'm very sorry, but I really don't see . . .'

'So far, I have kept my word. I am, as you know, not an indiscreet man. I had every intention of keeping his secret for ever. But I am also a man who will use every weapon at his disposal to keep his family together, intact, and I tell you this, Celia. If you persist in this obscene liaison, the price you pay is that I will tell the world about the conversation I had with Norman. I will shout the story from the roof-tops, and I imagine with what joy the Bishop would receive it.'

'But you can't. Anyway, what could you prove?'

'My darling, Norman is not a hardened member of the Mafia. He would hardly continue to lie if confronted with this story publicly. He would lose his position here and most probably — what is that picturesque phrase? — he would be defrocked. He and his family — Jamie's family — would be cast upon the tender mercies of the dole queue. My dearest Celia, what a wedding present you would make them.'

'Hunter, this is wrong. It's wicked.'

'Most probably it is,' he said with a smile. 'But it is what I will do, to keep you. Leave me for this boy and it will cost you your own children and the ruin of his family. Is that what you want Celia? Is what you get up to in the cave worth all that?'

Chapter 15

'It's a bit back of beyond,' said the boy with the bright face and the prison haircut.

'It's a dump,' said Dorothy sourly. She was drinking a tomato juice and eating crisps, while the boy, in common with the rest of the folk group, tucked into pints of Special and Frank and Brenda's scampi. Dorothy and the boy — his name was Ben — took their drinks and went over to the far side of the pub garden and stared out at the hills. In the uncertain light, everything had a sheeny quality; a pearl mist lay over soft yellows and greens and the distant blue of the hills was like satin. A wasp buzzed idly, attracted by Dorothy's drink.

'I guess it's quite pretty,' said the boy, 'if you like that sort of thing.'

'Just try living here,' Dorothy said. 'Where're you from, anyway?'

'Oh, we live in Swansea. Bill — my dad — pretends to be Welsh. I'm at Liverpool Poly at the moment, I'm on vacation.'

'Doesn't sound like you're having much fun.'

'This is my holiday job. Bill lost his licence earlier this year so I'm driving the band around. Folk Festivals and stuff. Bloody boring.'

'God. Bor-*ing*.'

'Right. Still not for long. I've been saving up. Next week I'm off, to Portugal.'

'Sounds great,' said Dorothy longingly.

'Come with me.'

'Har-har.'

'No, I mean it.'

'We don't know each other.'

'We would though, time we got home.'

'Oh, *yeah.*'

'Listen, I mean it.'

'What, really?'

'Yeah. Come with me.'

'My dad wouldn't let me.'

'He couldn't stop you. How old are you, eighteen?'

'Sixteen,' she said dourly.

'Still, he couldn't stop you.'

'I haven't got any money.'

'I've got money.'

'Yeah, but . . .'

'You think I'm joking, don't you?'

'Course you are.'

'I'm not. Promise. Let's go to Portugal. It'd be great. Shit, how I hate this macho beer. Think I'll get myself a coke. How about you?'

'He'll be with you soon, Mrs Green,' said the bearded man.

'Actually, it is Professor,' Daniel's mother said sourly. She was not in a good mood.

The man smiled at her as though he viewed her through a mist. 'Do sit down and make yourself comfortable.' The room, huge and Victorian, designed to be cluttered and stuffed, had been cleanly gutted. Light shone through an uncurtained bay window, parquet stretched in a glitter like a chill sea; the walls were white and empty, except for a poster over the empty grate which showed a child in a field of daffodils. A plain cross stood on the mantelpiece.

Professor Green had arrived at the Fellowship House in Llanafon.

'Hallo, mother.'

'Daniel!' But was it Daniel? He wore a smile that was unfamiliar. And yet familiar, too. Casting around in her recent memory, Professor Green dredged up the congruity; it was the smile of the man who had greeted her at the door. Beside Daniel, stood Anita, fresh and glowing in the pale yellow of sunshine.

He gave her a kiss — perfunctory — (though what young man is anything but perfunctory to his mother in public?). She tried to take hold of his hand, but somehow, he disentangled it.

'So nice to meet you, Mrs Green,' Anita said smiling. It was the same smile. Professor Green flinched from the outstretched hand. 'Professor Green,' she said, though she did not very often stand on ceremony. Like the bearded man, Anita did not seem to register the correction.

'Bit of a surprise to see you here, mother,' Daniel said.

'Daniel, we do not hear from you. And then when we hear, what we hear is so strange.'

For a moment, Daniel seemed at a loss. He opened his mouth, but before he could speak, another girl came in, dressed in pink and carrying a tea tray. 'Grub's up!' she sang. 'I'm sure you'll all be glad of a cuppa! Daniel, is this your mother? So pleased to meet you, Mrs Green.'

The Professor gave up. 'It is nice to meet you too,' she said without sincerity. The girl in pink also had the smile. Radiant was the word you would use to describe such a smile. All were smiling radiantly. Why, then, did it make her feel so cross?

'Shall I be mother?' said Anita.

'Thank you,' said the Professor. 'Milk and no sugar, if you please.'

'Of course, I don't have to ask how *you* like it, Daniel.' Anita put in, correctly, two spoonfuls of sugar and handed

155

it to him. The Professor observed the intimacy between the two of them, and she began to feel chill. 'Daniel, please you must explain to me why you are no longer at Mr Hunter's.'

'Do try some cake,' said Anita. 'This is coffee sponge. It's absolutely yummy.'

'I go first to Mr Hunter's and what do I find?'

'Cake, Daniel?' said Anita.

'No thanks.'

'Oh, go on, just a bit. I can't be greedy all on my own, can I?'

'Daniel . . .' said his mother.

'Well, just a bit.'

Anita put a large slice on Daniel's plate. '*There* you are. Must keep your strength up. Mrs Green, are you sure?'

'Quite sure. Daniel, I . . .'

'It's my favourite, coffee. I wish I could bake like Sue. Still, one day. Now, Mrs Green, I expect you're wondering what sort of a place this is that your son's got himself mixed up with?'

'Miss . . . er . . . Anita,' said the Professor. 'My son and I have things to discuss, privately. If perhaps you wouldn't mind . . .'

Daniel looked at Anita. 'Oh, no, please go ahead,' Anita said soothingly. 'Daniel and I have no secrets from each other, do we Danny?' She took a mouthful of cake. 'Oh, yum yum. I'm so greedy, but I can't help it, I'm afraid, I do love my little tummy. Sorry Mrs Green, I was interrupting you. Do please carry on.'

The Professor had just been given permission to address her own son. She took a deep breath and tried to describe the strange and dismaying encounter she had just had at Disserth House. 'I arrive at the house and I knock at the door, and there comes I suppose this man Mr Hunter to answer it who I hear is so good with the young. But today he is cross and not at all good with anyone. He stands at the door — I am not even asked in, though I have come all this way. He tells me that you have *not obeyed* his instructions, that you leave without his consent and he is no longer responsible for you. Daniel, what does this mean? What dreadful disobedience is this?'

'I think perhaps I can explain, Mrs Green,' said Anita. 'You see, I don't think that Mr Hunter approves of my friendship with Daniel.'

'I see,' said the Professor faintly. 'And why, please, should he not approve?'

Daniel and Anita looked at each other and then both broke into the sudden laughter of those who share a secret. 'Oh, I'm used to people not approving of me,' said Anita. 'It doesn't worry me at all.'

'Yes, but *why* does he not approve? What is there to disapprove of here? I must know.'

'This is a Christian community, Mrs Green. We have promised our lives to God. In these troubled times, that is sufficient reason for people to hate us.'

Professor Green turned to Daniel, attempting to continue her narrative. 'Well, Mr Hunter goes away. I think he will leave me standing there, in the middle of nowhere. But then a woman comes — Mrs Hunter, I suppose. She looks like a frightened mouse. She looks like a ghost. Oh, Daniel, she says, yes, he has gone. And she gives me your address. Then she scuttles away. What kind of a house did we send you to? Are these people mad? What is going on there?'

'Well, you see . . .' Daniel started, but Anita interrupted.

'I don't think we ought to talk about it, Mrs Green, if you don't mind. Let's just say that there were some very unsuitable goings-on, and we thought it much better that Daniel should be safely here with friends.'

'Then if Daniel no longer wants to be at Disserth House, perhaps this is a good thing, but then it is best if he comes home with me. I am grateful that you have been kind to my son, Anita, but now he should come home.'

Again Daniel and Anita looked at each other and laughed.

157

'Oh, no, mother,' said Daniel. 'I'm not coming home.'

'But darling . . .'

'I'm sorry if you came all this way for nothing, but really you shouldn't have bothered. I'm quite all right.'

'It's always hard, isn't it,' Anita said reassuringly, 'for a mother to face the fact that her children are grown up and no longer need her?'

'It is nothing of the sort. Daniel, I insist that we have a private conversation somewhere.'

'Especially when it's an only son,' Anita continued.

'Do you not think a private talk would be best? We could sit in my car perhaps.'

'Knowing that she just has to let go and let him get on with his own life . . .'

'Daniel, are you listening to me?'

But Daniel merely sat there, smiling.

Chapter 16

Would it rain, or would the sun shine? Mrs Woosnam went for sun, Mrs Potter, who tended to pessimism, said rain. By two thirty that afternoon the day still seemed undecided. Piles of pewtery clouds strove with islands of glittering blue. Sometimes the clouds won; the air darkened and a chill wind ran through all the long grass in the meadows, or else the sun came out and the world blazed into warmth.

'A pity if it rained all over your lovely flowers,' said Mrs Woosnam.

'I don't know about lovely; they're about to drop. Oh, dear. Look at her.' Both women stopped to watch Celia emerging from the gates of Disserth House.

'I think I'll step indoors a minute,' said Mrs Woosnam. It's gone a bit chilly. Join me, will you?'

'Right you are,' said Mrs Potter.

By quarter to three, things were beginning to happen. The band returned from the pub and parked the battered van in the sloping field that ran between graveyard and stream. Trays of bridge rolls, jelly trifles in waxed dishes, fairy cakes and jam tarts were carried over to the church hall. If Celia looked paler and more washed-out than usual, then she was so usually pale and washed out that it passed without comment, except by those — the news had not yet reached the entire community — who knew her to be a guilty woman. They, expecting to find the mind's construction in the face, thought it only right that bad Celia should not be looking well.

At ten to three, the girl from Woman's Hour arrived in a white Mini with her portable tape-recorder. She was pleased with the appearance of Hunter, whom she had interviewed five years before — he seemed to have grown more patriarchal, more Jove-like in the interval, his chest broader, his hair more resplendently silver. That he spoke to her as from a great height, biting off his words impatiently, seemed only appropriate. At ten to three, it seemed likely that the sun would shine.

At five to three, Professor Green, travelling along the Llanafon–Hereford road, and still shell-shocked from her encounter with Daniel, saw a lone black man trying to hitch a lift. Something desolate and alien about his demeanour made her pull in by the side of the road and call, 'Where did you want to go?'

'Come along now, chaps!' exhorted Deirdre Loftus. 'Stir your stumps! We're going to be late.'

'Look, ma,' said Jamie, 'perhaps I won't come after all.'

'What do you mean? Of course you'll come.'

'Quite honestly, it isn't really my sort of thing.'

'It's not Daddy's sort of thing, nor mine either, come to that, but we're going along. Flying the flag, putting St Rhuna's on the map!'

'Surplice, surplice . . .' sang Norman coming into the room.

'Hanging up in the scullery, all clean. Now come along, do.'

'Although whether one should be wearing the robes of Christianity for a pagan occasion . . .'

'Too late for that now! Anyway, you're the one who's always on about the sanctity of tradition! Do hurry up. Heavens, you're not going to take that dreadful old plastic bag, are you? Jamie, give Daddy a hand.'

'Ma, I really think . . .'

'Come along now everyone! Chop chop!'

'Really boring,' said Dorothy to Ben, 'all this old stuff.'

'Never mind. Come the revolution.'

Around the van, the band members were swigging glasses of Special and singing a song about a maiden and a coal-black smith. By present-day standards of rudeness, the song was not really rude at all, but they sang it as if it were.

'They're pissed,' she said. 'Do they always get pissed before they sing?'

'Before they sing, before they do anything. They're so old; they need artificial stimulation.'

Dorothy giggled. 'And do you?'

He looked down at her and grinned. 'God, no. *God!*'

Walter Jones and Mrs Walter Jones were wearing their Sunday best. Mrs Jones had been unable to persuade Kevin to wear his Sunday best too. She thought Kev seemed a bit peaky today, and wondered whether he might not be sickening for something. Still, at the moment, her mind was occupied with watching her husband flirting with the girl from Woman's Hour. Daft old thing, she thought regarding him with affection, doesn't he know he's a bit old for that sort of thing now?

'Tell me,' said the Woman's Hour girl, 'there must have been some very interesting local customs here when you were young.'

Mrs Walter giggled behind her hand.

'Oh, aye,' said Walter. 'Plenty of 'em.'

'Could you tell our listeners about some?'

'Most of 'em weren't the sort of things you could talk about,' he said. He leered at her.

The girl bridled in delight. 'Fascinating! Tell me more!'

★

'Hallo, Hunter, sorry we're late, we all got into a bit of a tiz; what hopes do you hold out for the weather? Oh, look, that girl with the tape-recorder; she must be your bod from the radio; how *exciting*.'

'Hallo, Deirdre. Ah, Norman. Well done. Let's go to the vestry, shall we? Oh and by the way,' he said to Jamie as if it were an afterthought, 'Mrs Hunter left this, for you.'

'Why, you old devil,' said Mrs Walter. 'What do you want to go telling her all that stuff for? Spring fertility rites indeed!'

'Well, it was what she wanted to hear, wasn't it?' said Walter. 'They think just because you live in the country, you must be daft.'

'What do you think everyone's doing now?' said Daniel, a little wistfully.

'Why?' said Anita. 'Do you really care?' She laughed. 'You soft old thing! Now come and give me a hand with these newsletters. We won't let you sit around dreaming while you're here, you know.'

Kevin, mooching around like the lonely adolescent he usually had no time to be, looked through narrowed eyes towards where Dorothy and Ben were laughing together by the van. Well, bloody hell! He'd show her! He'd show all of them.

'I've got a bit of a headache,' Celia said. 'It might be a migraine, actually.'

'Why, poor old thing!' said Deirdre. 'And today of all days! I've got some aspirins in my bag if they'd help.'

'I don't think they would, thank you very much.'

'We can't go together, you wally,' said Dorothy. 'This lot would put two and two together in no time. No, I'll go off first, and you slip away in a bit. It's not difficult. Go down the road till you get to a blue gate. Then follow the path down to the stream. I'll be waiting there, by this big tree. No one'll come looking there, I promise.'

'Pity about Mother, though,' Daniel said. 'I didn't like sending her away like that, really.'

'She'll come round in time, I expect,' Anita said cheerily. 'Pass the paperclips, would you please?'

'I'm not so sure she will.'

Anita put her sheaf of papers down and faced him squarely. 'Daniel, we all have to make sacrifices. *He that loveth father and mother more than Me is not worthy of Me.* Now, are you going to put Jesus first, or are you not?'

'Oh, yes, definitely,' said Daniel. He almost believed it. A little maggot of rationality still gnawed away, but it would not be there much longer.

Jamie, reading and re-reading the short letter, remembered Hunter's smile as he had given it to him. The smile had not seemed sinister at the time, but as he reconstructed it in his memory, it became like a smile in a bad dream. The letter was typed, but it was Celia's signature all right. Where was she now? People called out to him as he searched for her in the wide field and in the graveyard. People were everywhere now. Hunter's ceremony looked set to be a great success.

'The outlook today,' said the man on the three o'clock news, 'is unsettled. Thunderstorms are expected over Wales and the North and drivers are warned . . .'

The band, still knocking back Special, started on 'The Foggy Foggy Dew'.

The girl from Woman's Hour spoke into her microphone, 'I'm standing,' she said, 'in the little eleventh-century church of St Rhuna's with its quiet charm which

163

seems to embody the epitome of the English countryside oh fuck I forgot this is bloody Wales, isn't it, start again, Valerie, I am standing in the little eleventh-century church of St Rhuna's with its quiet charm which seems to embody the epitome of the British countryside. Yet life here has not always been so peaceful . . .'

The door opened and in burst Deirdre. 'Oh, hallo dear,' she said, 'don't mind me, I was just looking for my husband, last seen vanishing in the general direction of the vestry. Ah, there he is. Don't miss the font, dear, will you, it's Celtic.'

The Woman's Hour girl pulled a face at Deirdre and the font and started again.

'Oh, gosh,' said Celia, who had just come in by the other door, 'I thought . . . I didn't know . . . I'm sorry . . .'

'Don't be,' said the girl coldly. 'I was just off, anyway.'

Jamie caught up with Celia in the path that ran round the back of the church, the empty north side, the devil's side. It was a dank spot, shaded by a huge and knotted yew where the rubble of the churchyard was piled, broken grave-stones, green-scummed jam-jars, dusty marble wreaths.

'For God's sake, Celia,' he said, 'we have to talk.'

She stared at him in the undersea gloom as though she were terrified of him.

Chapter 17

'What I do not understand,' said Professor Green, as they drove through winding lanes, 'is how he can change so much in so few weeks. Somebody has been influencing him, I tell myself, but who? Is it this Mr Hunter? Or this woman? Daniel has never before been interested in girls; how then does this one suddenly accomplish so much?'

Joseph listened in polite silence. Up till now, the fate of Daniel, whatever it was to be, had not caused him much heartsearching, but now he saw he must revise his thoughts for the sake of this nice lady.

'Or is it us? Have we gone wrong somewhere? I ask myself again and again, but I can find no answer. Look, here is a pretty café. Shall we stop and have some tea? I feel thirsty enough to drink a river. Perhaps it is all these bad feelings.'

They were in England now, a village of jumbled black and white houses, a real village, with a green, a war memorial, an antique shop and a church with a Victorian piecrust frill up its spire.

'This is quite fine,' muttered the Professor automatically as they stepped down into the narrow doorway. 'Fifteenth century I should say at a guess. Do you see the cruck frame? What did you say you read at Oxford Mr Agbodeka?'

She was the first person he had met in England who had bothered to remember the correct pronunciation of his name. Joseph was touched and shamed. 'Bus timetables,' he said. 'The *Daily Mirror*, the Yellow Pages. Offers of two toothpastes for the price of one.'

'Here, by the window?' she said. 'Yes, what did you say?'

'You are a good woman,' he said humbly, 'and I cannot even afford to buy you tea.'

'I can always manage tea for a student. I can remember not so badly being young myself.'

'I am not so young,' said Joseph. 'Like Hamlet, I am older than I seem and less foolish.'

The Professor leaned back and looked hard at Joseph across the tablecloth. 'Mr Agbodeka,' she said, 'would you like to talk about it?'

Joseph sighed. 'It is a long story. And not I fear an edifying one.'

'We have plenty of time. And I have a hide like a rhinoceros, or so my husband is always telling me.'

'You mustn't keep following me around like this!'

'Then talk to me, for God's sake!'

'I can't. I *can't*.'

'Celia, what's happened?'

'Not now!'

'When, then?'

'I . . . I don't know . . .'

'How did he find out?'

'Someone saw us, Daniel Green, I think. Does it matter?'

'*He* made you write this stuff, didn't he? *You* never wrote this.'

'No . . . yes . . . I don't know. Look, I have to go.'

'I'm not going to let you, not till you tell me.'

'I can't tell . . . I mean there's nothing to tell . . . oh, Jamie, just go, will you?'

'Celia, do you think for a moment I'm going to let it all finish like this? He's found out! So what? It doesn't make any difference. We'll change our plans. We can go tomorrow if you like. Today! We can go today! Listen, there's a London train at six. Get the kids, do a bit of packing and meet me in the . . .'

'Jamie, you don't understand.'

'I'm trying to understand! It's you, you won't tell me what's happened. Why can't we go away today?'

'Because . . . oh, it isn't as simple as that.'

'Celia, has he been hurting you? Has he touched you? Because if he has, so help me, I'll . . .'

'No . . .' Her voice faltered. 'He doesn't need to . . . he doesn't do things that way . . .'

'Then for God's sake, what has he done? What has he said?'

'Well . . . he said he'd take the children away from me.'

'Of course he's going to say that! But you aren't going to believe him, are you? No one can take those children away from you, no one. You're a wonderful mother, anyone can see that.'

'No, it's not just that.' But what it was, Celia thought, she couldn't say. How could she tell Jamie what Hunter had just told her? Oh, Hunter was clever all right.

'Celia, you haven't . . . you haven't gone off me, have you? You do still love me?'

'Of course I do, but . . .'

'Then that's all that counts. Look, you're going to leave him anyway, so what, so you just leave sooner rather than later, Celia, listen; Celia, look at me, why won't you even look at me? This is killing me, you know that?'

'Scuse Oi,' said a large drunken member of the band, pushing past them. 'There a toilet anywhere here?'

'I don't think so,' said Celia. 'Please . . .'

'Bugger that then,' said the man, and went off into the nettles singing, 'Two, two the lily white boys, dressed up all in green ho ho . . .'

'Celia!' Jamie pushed his face close to hers. It looked unfamiliar, full of emotions she did not recognize. Just for a moment, it was almost as though he were the one she hated, so desperate was she to get away and sort out what had happened to her. Then the drunken man came back. 'Pissed all over the bloody nettles, didn't I?' he said. 'Not my fault if there's no bloody toilet.' As he shouldered himself past, and Jamie tried frantically to shove him out of the way, Celia took her chance to escape and darted back to the crowds gathering in the churchyard, where she would be — it was the word that occurred to her — safe. She could hear the drunk singing behind her, 'One is one and all alone and ever more shall be so . . .'

'Well,' said the Professor, 'it is not the worst story I have ever heard, not by a long chalk.'

'I have lied and I have cheated,' said Joseph mournfully. 'I have betrayed my family and squandered their hard earned money. I have wasted my life.' Even as he spoke the words, he could not help admiring something about them, their sonorous flow, the way they linked him with the grand tragedies, with Macbeth, with Charles the First on the scaffold, with Sidney Carton. They resonated, as if into a huge auditorium and then were stilled.

'Nonsense,' said the Professor briskly, 'you were backed into a corner from which you could not emerge without loss of face. Family expectations can be very cruel. I think I understand that now. If we had not expected so much from Daniel, perhaps he would not have fallen into the arms of this religious fanatic, but there you are. I cannot undo twenty years of perhaps doing the wrong thing all of a sudden. And you, too, you were under intolerable pressure, I think. With the expectations of your mother and sisters upon you, how could you have behaved otherwise?'

Joseph's tragedy shrank at once, from a grand histrionic one to one of smaller, more mundane proportions. Yet there was something very consoling about the Professor's words. He imagined a life which might be lived differently, a less exciting one, perhaps, but Joseph was tired; he wanted to stop running.

But he realized how impossible it was and rested his head on his hands in weary resignation. 'When you put it like that,' he said, 'it sounds so simple. Simple and forgivable.'

'Everything is forgivable,' said the Professor, 'except malice, and I do not think you are a malicious man, Mr Agbodeka.'

Joseph thought about this. No, he did not think he was either. Was there then hope for him? 'I did not expect any of this to happen to me. First you are the only person to stop your car for me all morning, and then you make me feel that I am not altogether a lost soul. I think, Professor Green, you must be some kind of a saint.'

Professor Green beamed at him. He was the only person that day to have got her name right, too. 'Far from it. But it takes someone who has made their own mistakes, I think, to be forgiving of them in somebody else. In the end, all is not to be abandoned. We are here, we sit drinking tea, we are civilized people.'

'Perhaps there is an answer for you,' mused Joseph. 'But I have no money, no job, and very soon, when they catch up with me, I will be in trouble with the immigration people. I will be deported; I will travel back in shame.'

'But perhaps there may be a chance for you,' said the Professor. She sighed a little, as she remembered the blank bright mindless smile on her son's face. That smile would haunt her through many nights. But she was a practical person. She had to be doing. If for the moment she could not help Daniel, then she would help someone else. 'Did you say you came from Kumasi? I don't suppose by any chance you are a speaker of Twi?'

'It's good to see you all here,' said the vicar smiling. The charming eleventh-century church was by now packed. 'Friends and strangers alike.' He smiled especially at Hunter and Celia, who between them might hold his fate in their hands. Celia had bought her clothes for the occasion weeks ago (that day in Shrewsbury, in fact, when she and Jamie had made love for the first time); a straw hat trimmed with pink flowers and a cream linen two piece. Today her face was the same colour as her dress. Those who still did not know wondered how a woman could wear new clothes and still look so dreadful.

'And now, let us think about the purpose of this ceremony,' Norman continued. 'Why are we here?' The expression on the faces of some of his congregation, including Walter, showed that they wondered that, too. 'Well, we are here to celebrate the miraculous life and death of a girl who showed how, in a wicked world, it is possible to lead a holy life . . .'

If he had not had his mind on other matters, Hunter would almost certainly have noticed that Dorothy was not there. Kevin noticed, though. He had watched her in tête-à-tête with the young man, and had seen them both going off, furtively, in the same direction, though at different times. He imagined what might be going on now between them. The thought of it made him squirm in his pew with lust. For the moment, his attention was diverted from another matter, which he should now have been thinking about.

'I hope that this ceremony, this celebration of innocence and virtue, having been revived at the instigation of our old friend John Hunter, will become once more part of the fabric of life in St Rhuna's as no doubt it was in the past. And so let us now sing the hymn "Come Holy Ghost", and afterwards we will all go into the churchyard for the Blessing of the Well.'

'Well,' said the boy. He gave a sigh, eased himself off Dorothy, and back into his jeans. 'What did you think of it?'

Dorothy considered. The act had not quite measured up to her wilder expectations of it, yet on the other hand, it certainly seemed worth another go. 'Yeah,' she said. 'It was really nice.'

The boy grinned. 'Never mind. The first time's often a bit of a let down. It gets better with practice.'

'Will we practice?'

'You bet. Plenty of time for that in Portugal.'

'Hey, you really mean that about Portugal, don't you?'

'Do I look like a liar? Still, I reckon you better get yourself on the pill or something before we go. Otherwise we might have a baby.'

Dorothy giggled. 'What will you do if I have a baby?' But she knew that the Lord protects the ungodly and the thought did not worry her too much. The boy seemed untroubled, too. 'Take it for walks,' he said. 'I like babies.'

'I hate them,' said Dorothy. 'There've been too many of them all over the house. God, I hate it here.' She yawned, adjusted her clothes and then suddenly rolled over on to her stomach, looking across at Ben. 'I've just thought of something. Can you give me a lift to the station?'

'The station?'

'There's a train to London in an hour. I could go and visit my ma in Brighton. While dad's busy. I'm sick to death of living with him and Celia.'

'London?' said the boy. 'We'll do even better. I've got these mates in London. We could go together. Then I could take you on to your mum's if you like, tomorrow, or the day after. Damian wouldn't mind. He's got this really huge flat. We'd have a big double bed all to ourselves.' He leaned across and kissed her. 'Get lots of practice in, then.'

'You mean it?'

'I told you, do I look like a liar? Go and pack your bag, and leave a note for your dad or whatever. I'll wait here.'

'But the van; won't you need to drive everyone back?'

'Sod that,' said Ben. 'I'm sick of them puking up and telling their dirty stories. They can get themselves back to Swansea. 'Sides, dad hasn't paid me yet. I reckon he owes me something.'

'You really mean,' said Dorothy, 'I can get out of here?'

'I told you,' said the boy. 'Now hurry up and get a move on before it rains.'

'It's a good thing they didn't lay tea in the open,' whispered Mrs Potter to Mrs Woosnam.

'Looks like we're going to get soaked any minute,' agreed Mrs Woosnam. 'Thought I heard thunder.'

'Oh, I hate it when it thunders,' said Mrs Potter. 'It goes up and down the valley. You get so frightened.'

Celia, standing behind Hunter at the flowery arch of the well, felt as though her head had been kicked in. Soon it would start to hurt, but at present, she just felt numb. Jamie had gone, after one more futile and angry attempt to talk to her. Hunter stayed, of course; he would not run away. He was impassive, though she could feel the anger running through him as he stood before her.

The worst had happened, she knew that, though she barely understood it. Yet already part of her mind was at work, processing the fact that her happiness was over.

Now that Hunter had laid down the rules, it did not seem that there could ever have been another way. The Celia who had lain in the arms of her lover and plotted to escape with him was another Celia, someone in a story perhaps, or in a dream. For the real Celia, there would be no such outcome. She was not meant for such things. That was all; it was almost a relief to recognize it.

Some lives were just not meant for happiness. She had to accept that and live the rest of her life accordingly. The rules could not be rewritten.

For the moment, she could not think of what she had lost. Just now she could not even picture Jamie's face. For the moment, the weeks of love and whispered secrets, of unimaginable joy, had gone, as though they had never existed. To survive, she must blank them out. She must return to being simply Hunter's wife, Hunter's woman. She must face a life lived by Hunter's rules, doing things Hunter's way. She felt now as though she had always realized it must be so. You could not win against Hunter, just as Adam and Eve could not argue with God against His sentence of banishment. God wrote His own rules and punished transgressors; and so did Hunter. God might behave badly, but in the end that didn't count; He would still win, and it was the winning that counted.

All Celia's life, Aunt May, her father, her schoolteacher lover, her depressions, the suicide attempt, giving birth, her unhappiness and the startling unexpected joy of Jamie, all these things became suddenly flat and undimensional compared to what she now saw was the one important fact in her life.

Hunter.

What might the years ahead be like? She could not begin to imagine them. They would be bounded by Hunter, they would be defined and edged and framed by Hunter. He would be in the background, the foreground, at the end of each perspective, the huge figure dwarfing the foreground, the tiny one standing aloof on the horizon. If she behaved, he would be nice to her, if she did not, he would not be. It was all one to Hunter.

The angel with the fiery sword stood on guard, but it was the way out he was blocking and not the way in.

Celia was to be trapped for ever inside the garden.

And Jamie? He walked alone to the vicarage through miles of lanes, furious, young, hurt. He had been her lover — but now he was not. He had youth on his side. He would survive. He had to survive.

173

In the meantime, he tried to sort out what had happened. He ran the events round and round in his head, but could make no sense of them. Already, he had begun to rewrite the story from the beginning. So Celia had never loved him. So she had been fooling with him all the time. You read about married women who behaved like that. They said women were weaker than men, didn't they? He would have braved all for her. He would have hazarded everything. He — who had little after all to lose — would have lost all for her. Why wouldn't she risk the same for him? And now a line that he had read and dismissed scornfully when he read the book of Donne's poems came back to haunt him. As he marched down the lanes, its rhythms rang scornfully in his ears. *Swear — Nowhere — Lives a woman, true and fair*. Celia, Celia. He would have been true, why couldn't she? *Though she were true when you met her — And last till you write your letter — Yet she — Will be — False ere I come to two or three* . . . In Jamie's troubled and bewildered mind, he saw Celia, just for the moment, as Hunter saw her, weak, treacherous, fickle.

As for Celia, caught in the garden, here was her life. She would simply have to get on with the living of it.

'It will not be so impossible,' said the Professor. 'I am always arranging for foreign students to work in this country. It is essential work. A translator for these tapes cannot be found — now you appear. You are the obvious person. Mind, I cannot promise that it will be interesting work, or that it will last forever.'

'But it is a thousand thousand times better than nothing. And nothing is all I had this morning. I shall be able to write and tell my mother that I am a research assistant at London University, and I will be telling the truth. You cannot imagine what this will mean to me.'

'Nonsense,' said the Professor gruffly. 'It suits both of us. And as I say, there is always our spare room. Of course, when Daniel comes back . . . yes, well . . . but until then . . . you are most welcome. I miss most dreadfully having a young person about the house.'

'You are a good woman,' said Joseph humbly. 'I do not deserve such goodness.'

'Oh stuff and rubbish!' said the Professor.

While the clouds gathered and Mrs Potter looked nervously at the sky, Hunter started his reading from the *Life Of St Rhuna*. He spoke in a resonant, deep voice that made you think he would have made a very good actor. 'Now the holy virgin came to the church to pray to God, and while she was there, Rhodri Ddu saw her and was inflamed with desire. He seized her and would have possessed her, but she, crying out, said that she would suffer no man to take her virginity from her.' Here Hunter paused and looked round at his audience. By now quite a few people in the crowd knew what had been going on. But Jamie was only a boy, and what did you expect from a boy? A boy would take whatever was going, anyone knew that. It was Celia they all blamed, standing downcast in her flowery hat and bridal suit. Hunter, meanwhile, continued, 'Yet he would not desist, whereupon she said she would rather die than be defiled. But he, taking his sword, struck her and slew her. But lo, where her head touched the ground, there sprang up straightaway a well, wherein were done many wonders, so that now the place is called St Rhuna's Well . . .'

Norman, ignorant of the abyss on which he stood, gazed into the well with an amused toleration, as he busied his mind with a debate about the possibility of St Rhuna's existence. If you extracted the fabulous elements from the story, you were left with a Dark Age anchoress who might very well have existed, and why not celebrate her sanctity? It was, he thought, a very beautiful, peaceful place here, in which there could now be very little evil left.

But at that moment, there was a commotion the other side of the churchyard by the gate. A blue car had stopped and a man waved his arms and shouted. The children, who were bored anyway, were the first to get there, followed by the band and then everyone else.

'Fire!' someone called. 'There's a fire!'

'Where?'

'Up the lane! Sounds like Walter's!'

'Is it bad?'

'Has someone phoned?'

'Where is it?'

'Walter's!'

In the confusion, no one noticed Kevin, who turned pale, then red. 'Bloody hell,' he muttered. 'Bloody hell! The bloody morons! They got the wrong bloody house!'

Chapter 18

It is seven o'clock in the evening.

And the thunder which has threatened all day has simply gone away; the evening sky is bright, and as the shadows lengthen down the valley, everything dazzles, glittering with prismatic light.

But the village has seen a tragedy today. If you drive past Walter's farm, you will feel the air still tainted by the damp, sour smell of the doused fire, see the desolate farmhouse, its once sparkling white walls streaked black and grey and yellow, the gaping blackness of windows, shattered glass, blistered wood, scorched paintwork. A chain of puddles in the yard reflects the pink iridescent evening light. No lives are lost, but as everyone in the village knows a house is more than four walls and a roof; the fabric of a family is irretrievably damaged. Mrs Jones has not yet begun to make a reckoning of all that has gone, her years of careful housekeeping gone to nothing; folded linen, polished brass, family photographs, baby clothes, Kevin's old school reports, silver wedding presents still in their wrapping paper, her grandfather's bible; she will remember these things piecemeal over the next few weeks, and each remembered item will be a new bereavement. The village, too, feel those losses — Mrs Woosnam and Mrs Potter recall the brand-new kitchen, that finally and after years of nagging, Walter had recently had fitted for his wife; Deirdre laments the two-hundred-year-old Welsh dresser with its array of blue and white china.

But still, no lives are lost, and for that Kevin must be thanked. Kevin, the hero of the fire, who has rushed to his motorbike, kicked it into life, and roared away, lurching and bouncing dangerously, across fields and through gaps in hedges, over the rough ground to reach the house before anyone else. Clouds of smoke billow from the kitchen and wispy trails of it streak from the windows above, but as yet the flames have not really ignited. His sick grandmother is in the house; luckily her ground floor bedroom is a long way from the kitchen. Smashing a window to climb in, he finds her in bed half asleep, groggily just aware of the smoke licking under her door and the foul smell making her cough. He hauls her stick-thin body out of bed; she is old and she is ill, but she is a tough country woman and he manages to get her out of the window, just before the suffocating smoke fills her room, shivering in her pink nylon nightdress; meanwhile the other rescuers arrive and help them both to safety.

It is then that Kevin tries to rush back into the house. What does he seek? Everyone assumes that he goes for Patch, Mrs Jones's ancient, half-blind collie, who spends most of his time by the Rayburn. They have to pull him away, and it is only then that someone notices that his arm is badly burned. Meanwhile, a human chain is in action, filling buckets, directing the hosepipe, but by now the fire has become a monster. Fire engines arrive from Llanafon, the ambulance comes and takes away old Mrs Jones and Kevin.

Eventually, the fire is controlled, though very little is left of the Joneses' farmhouse but the shell. The barn stored with straw has not gone up and none of the stock or farm machinery has been damaged. But Walter does not believe in insurance; although the village will help with benefit evenings, and whip-rounds, the fire is a disaster for him.

It is Celia who looks after the old couple (the Joneses have never before struck anyone as an old couple, but now they appear so), taking them to the hospital in Llanafon and then to the house of Glenys their married daughter, where she stays with them, until she is sure of their comfort. She has rallied round wonderfully that evening, not sparing herself. A little gloss is breathed upon the tarnish of her reputation, but only a little.

Hunter is wonderful, too, or at least, such is the impression he leaves. In fact, he has managed a combination of ubiquity and detachment, and if he has not actually put his shoulder to blackened beams, or hauled out damaged furniture, then nobody really expects it of him, any more than they expect such things of their silvery haired vicar. His expression, grim and remote, is only appropriate to the occasion.

So then it is not until seven o'clock, that everybody who is still there — the girl from Woman's Hour has long departed — gathers in the field beneath the church. The inappropriate planned celebrations, games, races and welly-hurling contests must now be abandoned. But still, something is needed to mark the events of the day; and so the band assemble and tune up their instruments.

The band, too, have been wonderful. For they, miraculously sobered, were among the first to spring into action, organize the human chain; they were the ones who dared go nearest to the blazing house. Now they are no longer strangers, but friends. They have names; Bill, Ozzie, Wally, Dic. (He spells it thus to show that he is no mere English Dick. He is one of them.) For the benefit of the villagers they abandon smiths and maidens and play the songs the villagers want to hear. They play 'Yesterday', they play 'Summertime', they play 'My Way'. They have not yet realized that their van has gone, and with it their driver; they will not do so until late that night, but with so many new friends, there can be no shortage of beds for them. What Hunter's feelings will be when he discovers Dorothy's absence is anyone's guess. He must, of course, be angry and hurt, too, for in his way, he loves Dorothy; but, luckily for Dorothy, his anger will be muted by the other discovery he has made that day. The mind, even Hunter's mind, can only absorb one betrayal at a time, and Dorothy is merely Peter to Celia's Judas.

There is another strange event that evening, whose significance, for the moment, is not realized. After the fire brigade have gone, a couple of police cars drive up to Walter's farm and several men, only one of them in uniform, spend a long time walking round the ruin and examining it. They measure distances and write down details on clipboards; they take away, in the bland speech of police reports, items for analysis. Still, Mrs Walter Jones was in the habit of leaving a dodgy old paraffin heater in the kitchen, because of a patch of damp in the back wall. Kevin warned her about this many times, but she took no notice. The chances are that the police, although they have their suspicions, will find no definite evidence, and anyway, why on earth should anyone want to burn down Walter Jones's farm?

For the time being, attention is distracted from the fascinating scandal of Mrs Hunter and the vicar's son, though it will still be there, to talk about in pub and living-room, over garden fence and cups of tea, for many months to come. People will look at Celia oddly and change the tone of their voices as she goes by; she will no longer find a friendly soul willing to look after the children for her, though, of course, now she will have less reason to leave them.

Tonight, though, the children — for this last time — have been swept up by Mrs Rees at Pentwyn Farm and are spending a pleasant evening with Julie and Gary Rees, eating fish fingers and watching television. Charlie, perhaps, might sense his mother's sadness, but for Amos and Rose, the crisis should pass unnoticed.

By seven o'clock, Celia has joined everyone in the field behind the church. She has spent a long time down by the stream weeping bitterly; now she is shaky, but in control. She thinks she has suffered as much as she can, but in fact, as she will realize over the next few days and weeks, she is still in shock and the flood has not yet hit her. For what must come is the full realization of how much she lives in a world governed by another; she must obey the rules or die. She thinks she will die anyway; she cannot see how she will endure. But that is rubbish, of course she will, and over the world human beings endure far worse things every day. For the moment, she does not — she cannot — think of Jamie. She must try and write him out of her life as though he had never been part of her story.

Wicked Celia. So you thought things could be different, did you? You thought you could write the words of your own life.

Wicked, foolish Celia.

Seven thirty. Two cars, one a smart Audi and another, a battered van, are approaching London. The Audi has already reached Westway, where the evening sky begins to glow with neon pink. When Joseph looks out of the window he sees many faces as black as his; he is no longer an exotic. Flyovers curve and sweep around him; the vivid flash of oncoming cars, Indian take-aways, car showrooms, furniture stores, he sees everything with the clear, heightened, sight of a man beginning a new life. He turns to look at the nice lady by his side. He is determined to be good.

A bit further back along the road, Dorothy and Ben talk and giggle, in the cool, apparently passionless tones of the young. They talk about the things they hate, and they discover, not surprisingly, though it seems wonderful to them, that they both hate the same things; flared trousers, hippies, Cliff Richard, the Royal Family. Ben tells her of the joys in store for her in London; they will watch television and go to McDonalds. She has never been to McDonalds, nor has she seen Dynasty. She thinks about making love to him. Another virgin has been lost to St Rhuna's. Dorothy looks forward to tomorrow.

In the churchyard, the arch of flowers has been crushed and the red and white petals of virgin and martyr are scattered and trampled. In the church hall, Mrs Woosnam heats water for the tea-urn; the men will lace their tea with whisky though they will not tell Mrs Woosnam that. The band is playing 'There'll be bluebirds over the white cliffs of Dover' and though they do not know the words, the older women do, and they sing in a mournful, keening quaver. A few couples even dance, though they have not danced for years. The evening sky is beautiful now, clear and un-polluted. The clouds are tinged with gold against pale, delicate blue. Instead of the aniline pink that Joseph sees, there is the faintest rosy smudge on the horizon where later the sun will set. But the evening is melancholy. Many of the villagers wipe away tears as they sing 'The shepherd will tend his sheep, the valley will bloom again . . .' and they remember the sorrows of their own lives, as they think of Walter and his wife. They remember relatives killed in the war, stillborn babies, dying husbands. They think of family emigrated across the world and never seen again, they remember plagues that have afflicted their flocks. Thinking of Walter's sorrow, all their sorrows become one.

Yet in world terms, really nothing of interest has happened; some small pieces of the pattern have been disturbed, and soon they will appear to be back into place. Even in the local papers, the fire will only rate a small paragraph, and at the Fellowship House, Daniel and Anita will not hear about it for several days. And the story of Hunter and Celia, of course, is private to them, though, of course, there will be local repercussions; people will speculate that the best thing Hunter can do is to take his penitent wife, and the remains of his family away somewhere else to start a new life. Perhaps if Celia is kept busy, she will not go astray again.

Anita and Daniel are looking out of the window at the Fellowship House.

'All that nasty thunder went away,' she says. 'I'm so glad. I asked the Lord to give us a nice day, and He did!'

'You know,' she goes on, 'when I look out of the window and I see all this lovely countryside and the hills and everything, I don't understand how anybody can be unhappy. Can you, Daniel? The Lord has been so good to us, hasn't he?'

Daniel agrees. Yet however hard he tries, when he thinks of the Lord, the face he sees is always Hunter's. This is not right, and he knows it.

'I can hardly believe I've been so lucky,' says Anita. 'Everything I've ever prayed for the Lord has given me. Here we are, you and I, just setting out on life's road, with so much to look forward to.'

Life's road. The Golden Road to Happiness. Daniel shoos Hunter's face away from his mind and tries to come to grips with Anita's words. The only image he can see is one which he knows comes from an advertisement; two children, hand in hand, facing an endless, bleak, diminishing perspective. It does not look exciting, and yet it must be. Life's road! He and Anita.

He still remembers with a pang of guilt a moment earlier that day when someone, who must have been himself, had briefly fancied Celia Hunter. Soppy Celia, adulterous Celia. How could he have done? Perhaps he did not do so at all. The memory begins to blur and to fade. There are a few more things that day that make him feel guilty, but it will soon be all right.

Anita breathes in the clean evening air. 'What's that

poem, Daniel? "God's in His Heaven, all's right with the world". Don't you feel just like that now?'

Well, yes, he does, Daniel thinks. At least, nearly. At least, if he doesn't now, he will soon. Any moment, in fact.